A Case of Mistaken Identity

He left the gym, but couldn't force himself to leave just yet. He liked the song the DJ had just pumped up. He stood outside, listening to the song's anthem that you couldn't trust anyone, not even your best friend.

He felt a hand on his arm and then a face coming close to his. He wasn't sure what was happening. Was it that dude who had threatened him earlier? Had Vince come out to whisper some naughty detail about the girl he had danced with? Was the face that of a vampire lowering its fangs toward his throat? His speculation stopped there. He felt a pair of lips lower and a slight suctioning of a kiss. The pair of lips brushed his throat.

"I was waiting for you," the girl purred. "You playing hard to get, or what?"

"You were waiting for me?" he asked meekly. He pointed a finger at his heart.

The girl let out a sharp cry when she realized her mistake. She had kissed not her intended lover boy but a stranger. She let out another cry, turned, and ran away.

The girl disappeared into the gym.

"Dang," he muttered. He sucked in his breath and could feel the cool minty taste on his lips. He repeated the action and was dizzy with wonder. It was a fresh experience, a kiss that made him breathless. He liked it—he liked it a lot—and now she was gone.

Help
Wanted

ALSO BY GARY SOTO

GARY SOTO

Help Wanted

STORIES

HARCOURT, INC.

Orlando Austin New York San Diego Toronto London

For information about permission to reproduce selections from
this book, write to trade.permissions@hmhco.com or to Permissions,
Houghton Mifflin Harcourt Publishing Company,
3 Park Avenue, 19th Floor, New York, New York 10016.

www.hmhco.com

First Harcourt paperback edition 2007

The Library of Congress has cataloged the hardcover edition as follows:
Soto, Gary.
Help wanted: stories/by Gary Soto.
p. cm.
Summary: Ten stories portray some of the struggles and hopes of
young Mexican Americans.
1. Mexican Americans—Juvenile fiction. [1. Mexican Americans—
Fiction. 2. Short stories.] I. Title.
PZ7.S7242H45 2005
[Fic]—dc22 2004007510
ISBN 978-0-15-205201-0
ISBN 978-0-15-205663-6 pb

Text set in Meridien
Designed by Linda Lockowitz

DOH 10 9 8
4500757216
Printed in the United States of America

In memory of Graciela Olivar,
a bilingual teacher who loved her students

Contents

Paintball in the Wild

Michael Ortiz wiped the steam from his eyeglasses and turned off the iron. He held up the top of his military uniform. The creases in front were sharp. He felt pleased with himself, a cadet in seventh grade and with the rank of corporal. He had been in cadets only since the beginning of school and by October he already had two stripes, plus three ribbons for drill, hall patrol, and conduct.

The conduct one was special because he used to be moody before he joined cadets. In sixth grade he sat through all his classes with his chin in his hand, his eyes half closed, and a yawn from boredom building up at the back of his throat. His grades were Cs and Ds. Sometimes he got into fights, but he usually thought they were just too much trouble.

Now he was a year older. His body said so. He was two inches taller.

"Sharp," he said to himself. The hot iron answered back with a sigh and a burst of steam.

He hung the shirt over his pants, already ironed, and pinned his ribbons back onto his uniform. He undid them when he noticed they were a little crooked over his shirt pocket. He petted the ribbons. He fogged the bars with his breath and polished them with a Kleenex, careful not to undo the creases on the front of his shirt.

When he heard his mother holler from the kitchen, he turned away from his uniform. *"¡Miguel! ¡Miguel, teléfonooooo! ¡Apúrate! ¡Ya! Tenemos que comer."*

Michael, born Luis Miguel, wished that his mom could speak English, but she was in her own world, a world that remained rooted in Mexico. He loved her deeply and would never tell his mother to please learn English like his father had. His father was so proud that he would stop at telephone poles just to read posters aloud in an accented mutter.

"Voy, Mami," Michael answered back.

He hurried out of his bedroom and took the phone from his mother. His nose twitched when he smelled breakfast—*papas* and *huevos con* weenies. The little weenies were marching in the fry pan. Breakfast was almost ready.

"Hey," Miguel said. It was Trung, his classmate

from Jackson Junior High and a corporal like himself but with one more ribbon than him—a bivouac ribbon because his platoon got to go camping and learn how to use a compass. Miguel made no bones that he was jealous of that extra ribbon on Trung's shirt. He had repeatedly told his friend that he would have gone on the weekend bivouac except his mother didn't like him staying at anyone else's house. When he'd tried to explain that they were camping outdoors, she still remained firm. That evening he pouted in his room with the lights out. Not even the sight of his uniform could perk him up.

"You gonna be ready?" Trung asked.

They were going to a paintball war in the foothills outside Fresno. He was going to tell their teacher, Mr. Mitchell, the cadet commander at school. Maybe this outing would count as a bivouac.

"Nine-thirty," Michael said. His eyes looked up at the clock over the refrigerator. "You gonna lend me the stuff?"

The stuff was a gun and goggles.

"Yeah, like I said." Trung reminded Michael that it cost twenty-five dollars, plus there were paintballs you had to buy. At least a thousand rounds were needed for the day. He also reminded him to bring drinking water.

"I got water," Miguel answered. Earlier in the week he had biked across town to an army surplus store and bought an authentic canteen. He liked that it was dented and imagined that bullets had ricocheted off its side. "And I got the money." A rich uncle from Los Angeles had sent him fifty dollars for his birthday.

Michael hung up the telephone. He stared at the frying pan, then at his mother, who asked, *"¿Dos huevos?"*

He held up two fingers, then saluted his mom—he just couldn't help himself. He was a military boy.

Michael sat in the back of Trung's father's truck, with his knees up to his chin. Although it was a sunny morning, he was cold in the whipping wind. He was wearing only a flannel shirt, flecked with paint that he figured would work as camouflage. His tennis shoes were also flecked with paint.

He turned to Trung. "It's cold."

"You should have brought a jacket," his friend answered. The collar of his own jacket was flapping like a sail.

"You didn't tell me." But Michael knew that was a poor defense. A cadet, he knew, should be prepared for all kinds of weather conditions. He was glad that he had brought water. He patted his canteen and touched the front pockets of his pants, where he had stashed candy bars and pumpkin seeds. He closed his eyes, wrapped his arms around his chest, and rode out the cold.

A half hour later the back window slid open when the truck pulled off Highway 41. Trung's brother, Truc, and his friend Tran, were in the cab, each of them cradling the gun barrel with one hand and fingering the trigger set on safety with the other. Truc said something in Vietnamese to Trung. Their father said something, too, and it sounded like he was angry.

"What did your father say?" Michael asked. They were approaching the paintball war ground called No Man's Land.

"He said be careful."

To Michael it sounded like a lot of words just to say *be careful.* In Spanish it was simply *cuídate.*

When the truck stopped, the two boys gathered their equipment and jumped out of the back, landing like ninjas. Michael felt ready for combat and was already searching the trees for snipers.

"Thanks, sir," he called to Trung's father, who was going fishing while the four boys went to war. Bright fishing lures hung from his vest like war medals.

Trung's father said something long and maybe angry at Michael. He grinned sternly and showed his ruined teeth. The truck pulled away, stirring up dust over the gravel road. The taillights flashed like gunfire when he braked at the end of the road. Then the truck turned left and was gone.

"What did your dad say?" Michael asked.

"He said that his father died in the war." Trung had shouldered his equipment.

It was too late to say that he was sorry. He didn't

know that Trung's grandfather had been in the Vietnam War. He saw Trung in a new light. Maybe Trung deserved that bivouac ribbon after all on account of his grandfather getting killed. Michael's own grandfather had gotten his foot crushed by a forklift, but that didn't count as much.

"Let's go," Trung said, with his hand already in his pocket, searching for the twenty-five-dollar admission. They approached the front office. A woman with a tattoo of a butterfly on her throat sold them tickets and six cartridges that held the paintballs.

"How about candies?" she asked. The butterfly on her throat seemed to flap its wings when she spoke. Her breath was anything but candy. It smelled sour.

Michael knew that the candies were overpriced. And he already had some candy in his pocket, enough to give his blood a good blast of energy. But he wanted to be friendly and said, "Okay." He bought a Milky Way.

Their hands were stamped and the four boys entered the gated area, where they walked down a dusty trail. At the end of the trail they came across three white men wearing T-shirts that said VIETNAM VETS. They were sitting on top of a picnic table, loading their guns. The men locked hard stares on the four boys.

¡Chihuahua! Michael thought. They're real soldiers. He had imagined that there would only be kids their age, but as they stepped into the wooded area he saw

more adults. For the first time, he felt scared. He took off his glasses, fogged the lenses with his breath, rubbed them clean, and put them back on his face. Two more men appeared out of the bushes, their faces painted green and black.

"How come there are so many grown-ups?" Michael asked in a whisper.

"They like it," Trung answered. "They get to be kids again."

It didn't make sense to Michael. But he had a bigger worry. "Does it really hurt when you're shot?"

Trung had told him that the paintballs did hurt, but he hadn't really believed him. Even when Trung lifted up his shirt and showed him the bruises. But then he was thinking that maybe they did hurt, like a rubber band shot at you at close range.

"Okay, newbie." Trung took Michael's gun away. He began to load it with a fifty-round cartridge.

Newbie was like *rookie*, and Michael didn't like the word. But he didn't say anything as he watched Trung load and then unload the cartridge. He handed the gun to Michael and said, "Okay, you do it."

He slipped in the cartridge, but struggled to take it out—he had to use a thumb to undo a latch.

"You'll be dead if you don't go faster."

"It's my first time!" Michael scolded.

"That's why you a newbie." He next explained how the game of paintball worked. You made teams of ten on each side, sometimes more, sometimes fewer. "If you get hit," Trung warned, "don't take off the goggles. Just stay still or you'll get hit again. Here you have to lie on your belly."

Michael swallowed. He had to ask again. "Does it *really* hurt to get hit?"

"Only in the leg." Trung then added that it hurt in the arms, too, and the butt. But you would deserve it if you got tagged in the butt. What was it doing in the air? Why were you running away? Only guys who ran away got tagged there.

"I ain't going to run away," Michael countered. But he could see himself running away. He could see himself dead in the field, a vulture picking at his entrails.

"Let's go, homey," Trung said after he attached the air hoses that supplied power to the gun.

Michael followed his friend. He lowered his eyes and watched his goggles swing on his chest—left, right, left, right—to the rhythm of his march. They were headed to the center of the field, where a paint-splattered flag hung limp as laundry. Trung told him that the object was to get the flag. The side that first pulled it from the ground was the winner.

Truc and Tran had skipped down earlier to the center of the field. They were smiling and eager to get started. But Michael, a cadet, was all business. For him war was war, even if it was paintballs and not bullets flying through the air.

"How many rounds do you got again?" Michael asked.

"Two hundred," Trung answered. "And you got fifty, remember?'

Doscientos, he wondered in Spanish. He saw in his mind two hundred bodies scattered across a field and a vulture on top of each one of them. With each tug of flesh, the vultures gripped harder and flapped their evil wings.

But he let the image go. He was about to ask why his gun held only fifty rounds, then he remembered he was using Trung's old equipment. Trung had every right to have the better gun.

The three Vietnam vets were in the center of the group, and one of them was attaching knee pads. He was trim, and his jaw was dark with a day-old beard. He stared at Truc and Tran, who said something in Vietnamese. The boys quieted, however, when the vet answered back in Vietnamese. He laughed at the boys and shaped his fingers into a gun and shot them.

The boys pretended they were shot. They laughed and raised their guns up at the vet.

"Don't point until we're on," one of the other vets snarled.

Truc and Tran lowered their guns.

Teams were made up. It was the four boys plus six high school kids, all friends in matching dark clothes, against the vets and seven other men. To Michael one man seemed as if he might have served in World War II. He was old; his front teeth and hair were gone. But he had ears, Michael noticed, and they were hairy. They were like earmuffs without being earmuffs.

Michael followed his squad and the barking of their leader. They immediately learned his command name: Squirrel. They headed two hundred yards up the hill, and the squad of older men headed in the opposite direction.

"Let's not get hit by friendly fire," Squirrel said, his goggles already down. His finger was already on the trigger, but the safety was locked.

Friendly fire, Michael thought. He had heard that before. "Friendly fire," he repeated under his breath.

"Distance yourselves," Squirrel ordered. "Don't bunch up, and let's be honest. If you get hit, don't wipe the paint off." He scanned his squad until they all wagged their heads in agreement. He then gave them each a code name.

"You!" Squirrel shouted. He was pointing at Michael. "Stay next to Turtle." Turtle was one of the high school kids and looked like a turtle with his head sunk down into his shoulders. Squirrel told the four boys that they each had a name—Bird One to Bird Four. Michael was Bird Three. He was glad that he wasn't Bird Four because that would have brought his confidence down. He didn't know Tran, but Michael hoped that he would be better than him at paintball.

Michael turned to Trung—Bird One—and had the feeling that he wanted to say good-bye. After all, wasn't this kind of like war? He licked his lips and undid his canteen from his belt. He felt foolish. He was the only one with a canteen; everyone else had water bottles stuck in their oversized pants pockets. He drank long and hard, and then placed his canteen in the loose soil.

"Everyone get their goggles down!" Squirrel ordered. "Connect your hoses if you haven't done so! Safeties off!"

Michael worked his goggles down over his eyeglasses. They fogged immediately. Squirrel, in frog leaps, advanced toward Michael. He took the goggles off Michael's head and said, "Spit in them, Bird Three!"

"What?" Michael asked, confused. But when he saw Squirrel's Adam's apple bob as he gathered a gob in his mouth, Michael immediately spit into his goggles. Squirrel told him to rub it in. That would stop the fogging.

A whistle cried. The battle was on.

Michael sat down in the leaves, his gun between his legs. He looked down at the valley where the wind stirred the flag. He could see movement in the brush and he heard the click of a gun safety. He then heard Turtle whisper, "Let's go!"

Crouching, he followed Turtle, and together they descended the hill that was worn bare from previous

wars. Michael looked to his right and saw Trung and
Tran following someone called Crow. They were moving smoothly, as if they were born to combat. *I'm not
jealous*, he thought—but he was, for he himself was
descending the hill mostly on his butt. Jealousy was
quickly supplanted by fear when he heard fire from
the other side—a paintball whizzed over his head and
hit a tree. Three shots hit in front of him. If he had
been in that place, he would already be dead, out of
the game. He was glad that he was slow, and glad that
Turtle was starting to return fire. Turtle had a gun that
spit rapidly.

"Bird Three," Turtle called. "Left flank, ten o'clock."

Michael thought, *Left flank, ten o'clock*. He knew
that they were military terms, but could only guess at
their meaning. He swiveled his head left.

Fifty yards away one of the Vietnam vets was
crouching near a granite rock. The vet's teeth were
shiny, a giveaway. He started to raise his gun.

"*Ay*," Michael muttered and backed away on his
butt. Dust rose up all around him.

"Shoot, Bird Three!" Turtle ordered. Turtle himself
was firing at movement in a bush. When the fire was returned, Turtle went down on his belly and crawled like
a turtle toward the bush. The smoke of dust rose around
his body. He stopped to wipe his dusty goggles.

Michael raised his gun and fired blindly, a round of
paintballs cutting through the air. The vet disappeared

behind the rock, still alive. The blood from his paint-balls dripped on the face of the rock. Michael, feeling a little braver, moved to his right down the hill. He looked back; he didn't want anything to do with the vet—for now.

Turtle and the guy in the bush were gunning for each other. Michael could see the guy from where he was. He was a man in black, a sort of ninja. Michael thought: *I can get him.* He began to duck waddle toward the man, who was pinned down by Turtle's fire. The firing stopped, and he could hear both Turtle and the man changing cartridges. Michael wondered if he should wait until the cartridges were in before he fired. He wanted to be fair. He counted to five—that was enough.

"Now," Michael said to himself.

Twenty yards away from the man, Michael fired and hit him—the paintballs exploded on his arm. The man let out a small chirp of pain and groaned, "Dead."

Michael wondered if the shots had hurt. They must have because the man was holding his arm. He looked over at Turtle, who was giving him a thumbs-up. Then Turtle's hand flattened in a sign to get down.

"Down!" Turtle blurted.

A Vietnam vet had sneaked up on them and started firing from behind a tree at Michael. But the vet stopped when Turtle fired from his position. The vet collapsed to the ground, unhurt, and crawled into a hole that was deep enough for a coffin.

Michael returned fire. Paintballs whizzed over the hole and exploded on the limbs of yellowish trees that appeared dead. He knew his fire was pointless, but his confidence grew every time he pressed the trigger. He liked the feel of the gun thumping in his hands. He liked the sight of the paintballs spitting out of the gun barrel.

Michael glanced over his shoulder. Turtle was moving swiftly toward the hole. Turtle motioned Michael to climb back up the hill and go around. Michael nodded and hurried away, his flannel shirt snagging on brush and tearing. His tennis shoes slipped in the dust.

"But he knows," Michael caught himself muttering. The Vietnam vet had been in a real war and knew that Turtle and he were going to try to flush him. The vet couldn't be that dumb, or could he? Michael had seen a lot of vets holding up signs in San Francisco that read: PLEASE HELP, GOD BLESS YOU. These men were gray-haired, with lined faces where their tears ran from the sadness of having no place to live. Pigeons pecked at their feet.

But Michael shook off this image. He was at war, and this vet was trying to tag him. He moved up the hill, stopped briefly to get a drink of water from his canteen, and then started down again. He stopped twenty feet from the hole and wiped his goggles on the sleeve of his shirt. He could see Turtle, who was down on one knee. He was wagging his head no.

They waited.

Michael could see action on the other side of the hill. Paintballs were flying wildly and little explosions of dust rose where the squads scampered behind rocks, brush, trees, and tree stumps. Two soldiers were on the ground, dead and out of the game. He thought of his friends, who probably were speaking Vietnamese among themselves. He wished he could say something, in either English or Spanish, but who was there to talk to? He reached into his pocket and brought out the Milky Way candy bar. When he tore off the wrapper, the candy was a flood of melted chocolate. He drained the gooey chocolate into his mouth and licked his fingers. So what if he swallowed dust? He was hungry.

"Ay," he muttered.

The shadow of a hawk scared him. And it didn't comfort him to see a lizard staring at him, its tongue like a lance. *Are these signs?* he wondered. And he had to wonder about his friends fighting against the Vietnam vets. Was Trung mad that his grandfather had been killed by the U.S. military? He didn't seem mad. In fact, Michael could make out Trung's laughter in the distance. Were he and the Vietnam vet taunting each other?

Then Turtle began to fire at the hole.

Michael jumped to his feet, gun raised. He advanced toward the hole, crouching, his shoulders tense. The vet swung around and shot toward Michael, but the paintballs whizzed past. Michael stopped, felt his heart thumping, and leaned against a tree. He swung away from the tree and launched an attack as he moved from one tree to another. The paintballs burst at the lip of the hole.

"Give up!" he heard himself say. Where did he get the guts to ask the enemy to surrender?

"You wish!" the vet hollered, and then returned fire.

Michael started to fire again, but his gun was empty. Michael brought out a new cartridge from his fanny pack and clipped it in. *Easy,* he thought. He began to once again pepper the hole.

The vet returned fire at Michael, and then swung around as Turtle came running toward the hole. They each shot at the same time, and both let out a chorus of "Ahhh."

Michael waited before he approached them carefully.

"You're both out?" Michael asked.

"For now," the vet answered. He was examining the red stain on his T-shirt. He had gotten hit two times.

Turtle was looking at his shoulder, where he had taken his hits. He seemed mad at himself. He dropped cross-legged and took a water bottle from his pants pocket.

Michael left the two and moved down the hill. He walked slowly, each step from heel to toe, as he headed toward the flag. When he was twenty yards from the flag, he heard Trung talking in Vietnamese. He thought he was addressing his brother or his brother's friend, Tran. But he was crowing with one of the Vietnam vets, who knew the language of his enemy.

"Weird," Michael muttered. He hurried over to Tran, who was sitting back and tossing corn nuts into his mouth. His gun was at his side, along with a sack of cartridges.

"What are they saying?" Michael asked.

Tran noisily chewed his corn nuts, swallowed, and rolled his tongue over his front and back teeth. "They're talking about where they bought their guns on the Internet," he answered. He tossed back a few more corn nuts.

Michael was confused. Was it okay to talk to the enemy?

Then there was firing from both sides. Tran was hit in his shoulder.

"Uhha!" Tran screamed, a half-chewed corn nut falling from his mouth. Michael thought at first that it was one of his teeth. He was going to ask if it really hurt when paintballs burst at his feet. He scampered down the hill and jumped behind a rock. He was breathing hard and sweat was washing over his face. His heart was thumping like a rabbit.

"I need a drink of water," he muttered to himself. But his thirst disappeared when he sensed movement in a bush. He turned and, without thought, shot a round. He saw an enemy—an adult, bending over in pain, holding his stomach. Between his fingers leaked purple paint.

"It does hurt," Michael remarked. The man had a gut that wobbled like Jell-O, and Michael figured that if the fat around *his* middle hadn't softened the blow, then how would Michael stand it? He touched his stomach. He wasn't looking forward to getting hit there.

He retreated halfway back up the hill, and rested for a moment as he looked down on the fighting. When he heard footsteps behind him, he galloped once again into the valley. He stayed hidden in a bush while the paintballs began to fly at one of his other squad members. He took off his goggles, something he had been told not to do, and wiped the sweat around his nose. He quickly put them back on—a sniper had located his position. He scrambled out of the bush to his right, where he believed Trung and Truc were battling.

Someone said something in Vietnamese. He knew it wasn't Trung or his brother because the voice belonged to a man. From behind a rock, he saw the enemy, those who had been knocked out, and a few of his squad members. He swallowed. On the ground, not too far from the flag, were Trung and Truc. Both were facedown, splatters of paint on their backs and around their armpits. A hawk swung in the sky, and its shadow touched both of them.

"Trung," Michael muttered under his breath. He squeezed his eyes shut. He imagined a vulture on Trung's back. The vulture was pulling a strip of flesh and raising his beak to get it down his throat. But Michael's eyes sprung open when he heard a branch snap. He saw movement in a bush. He rose to his feet and ran toward the figure, firing. The figure jumped from the sting of the paintballs, then dove into the cover of the bush.

"I'm down," a voice called from the bush. He sat in the dust.

Michael was breathing hard, sweat fogging up his goggles. He took them off quickly, wiped the sweat from the lenses, and put them back on. He gazed at his surroundings. He knew that most of his squad was down, even Squirrel, who was sitting with his arms around his knees. He was pulling foxtails from his cotton gloves. An empty water bottle lay at his feet.

Silence.

Michael could hear a car start up in the parking lot. He could hear a single-engine airplane. His senses were keen. He could even smell barbecue potato chips—someone was snacking on junk food before the next round of combat. His stomach rumbled. His ear twitched when he heard the flag snap. He was only twenty feet away. Three leaping steps, and it could be his!

Silence.

Sweat dripped down the sides of his nose. He tasted salt and something close to blood.

"I'm going to try," he told himself. He scanned the valley. There was no movement, except two hawks were circling above. He envisioned his cadet uniform to give himself strength. He saw a row of ribbons on his chest and a single medal for marksmanship. *Nah, make that bravery.*

He scrambled to his feet, finger on the trigger, and scurried to a tree, where he crouched, waiting for his breathing to calm and the pulse in his wrist to slow. He *was* tasting blood—the sun had caused his nose to bleed. He held his nose to his shirtsleeve until the blood flow stopped. He ran his index finger under his nostril—just crusted blood.

"You can do it," he told himself. "Win it for your squad!"

He stood up, mumbled, "You can do it," and shooed away the gnats that circled his face. He licked his lips, counted to ten, said, "Now," and dashed toward the flag.

A burst of fire from two directions hit him on all sides.

He let go of his gun, stung, and fell next to Trung,

who had rolled over onto his belly. His eyes were open, motionless.

"It hurts," Michael groaned.

Trung's eyes wouldn't move. He was playing dead for his friend.

Michael squirmed from the pain and then forced his body to be still, even as the nosebleed started again and rolled down the side of his cheek. If Trung could play dead, so could he. He pictured a vulture on his back and winced when he imagined the beak piercing his flesh. The pain was nothing, and his mom's crying next to nothing. He was a cadet. He pictured himself being lowered into the ground, a bivouac ribbon on his chest after all.

Sorry, Wrong Family

Carolina wrinkled her nose when her little brother, David, tipped a liter bottle of Dr Pepper into his mouth, swigged a little, and then sent the flavorful backwash of soft drink flowing back into the bottle.

"It's mine now," he claimed with a laugh that resembled a bark. He smacked his lips and burped. "But if you want some, you can have some." He pushed the bottle toward her.

"That ... is ... dirty," she said as she set her fork on the edge of her dinner plate. "Dad, did you see what David did?"

Her father's face was hidden behind the sports page. "The Dodgers lost three in a row," he mumbled.

"Dad, David spit in the Dr Pepper."

"David, don't do that no more." He showed his stubbly face from behind the newspaper, wagged a finger at David, and returned to the newspaper.

Carolina fumed at her father and her little brother. *We have no manners*, she concluded. She had intended to pour herself a glassful of Dr Pepper, but now she could only get herself a glass of water. She sighed. She lowered her head and surveyed her dinner of enchiladas, beans, rice, and salad. The salad, she saw, was scooted to the side of the plate. She had learned that salads required their own plate and recalled hinting at her mother that salads were served that way. Her mother, a bank teller who plied out money all day, had responded in a surly voice, "Not in this house. I'm not going to wash extra dishes."

Carolina stabbed at a wedge of tomato and fit it into her mouth as her mother returned from the kitchen, licking her fingers—a no-no in Carolina's book. It was a no-no in Miss Manners's book as well.

"Who was that on the phone?" her father asked.

"A telemarketer—how they bother." Her mother plopped down in a chair. She sized up Carolina's unhappy face. "What's the matter?"

Carolina had also learned that it was impolite to bring up complaints at dinner. It was better, she had read, to discuss the matter in private. "I'll bring it up later, if that's okay."

"No, it's not okay." Her mother balanced a weighty forkful of beans inches from her mouth. "Spill it, girl."

Carolina sighed. She could feel her mouth fall open at the sight of the beans being shoveled onto her mother's outstretched tongue, but her mouth reshaped itself into a gasp as her mother reached for the Dr Pepper. "Mom, I wouldn't drink that."

Her mother finished smacking the food in her mouth. She rolled her tongue over her back molars for a quick brushing. "I'm thirsty and I'm not on a diet. I can drink what I want."

"I just wouldn't, Mom." She eyed her little brother, who was kicking his legs and smiling a toothless smile— at age six he had lost his front baby teeth in an unnatural way. He had lost them when he bailed out from a tall swing and landed face-first in the dirt. "Because David drank from the bottle." She didn't bother to explain that he had spit some of the soda back into the bottle.

"Did you do that?" his mother asked.

David nodded. He chuckled.

"You precious rascal," she scolded lightly. "You're not supposed to do that."

When her mother uncapped the bottle, Carolina had to look away. Her eyes fluttered closed momentarily but reopened when she heard a burp.

"David, that's not polite," Carolina caught herself saying. She hoped that her new tactic, a caring, grown-up tone in her voice, might be a way of reaching her brother. True, David was only six and a brat. Still, he might learn.

David tried to kick her under the table. "That wasn't me, stupid." He stabbed an arm in the direction of their mother. His fingers were splayed like a pitchfork. "It was Mom."

"Mom!" Carolina scolded.

"What?" her mother nearly screamed.

"Burping?"

Her mother crushed her napkin in her fist. "You think you're high and mighty, don't you?" Anger swirled in her eyes as she bared her teeth. "High and mighty, Miss Too-Good-for-the-Rest-of-Us!"

Carolina picked up her dinner fork and parted the enchilada. She wondered what Miss Manners would do at such a moment. She could feel the heat of her mother's wrath. Before taking a bite, she opted for an apology and said, "I'm sorry."

"That's right, you're sorry." Her mother tore a tortilla and slapped one half down on the pile of beans. She snorted and said, "Sorry, sorry, sorry."

"But I said if we could talk about it later."

"Sorry, sorry—"

"Knock it off!" her father bellowed.

The three of them froze.

He set the newspaper down. "Can't we have a nice family dinner?" he asked. His jowls hung like pears on his face. His large Adam's apple rode up and down his stubbly throat, but he issued no more words.

"I made the enchiladas for you," Carolina's mother said. "Your favorite."

The squiggly line of his mouth moved around before it finally settled into a smile. "That's right, you did. Come on, let's chow down." He reached for the ketchup bottle. He squeezed the nearly empty bottle over his enchiladas. He pounded the bottle and then squeezed it one more time until it produced a rude sound that made David laugh.

Carolina's mother laughed, and her father laughed but stopped when he remembered that the Dodgers, a team he had grown up with, had lost three in a row.

Sorry. The word prompted Carolina to drag her sadness to her bedroom, where she opened her diary. She wrote: *I didn't like dinner. David spit into the Dr Pepper and Mom still drank it.* She told her diary about her day at school: Elena, her best friend, had scored a Perfect in spelling, and a first grader she didn't know came to school with his head shaved because of lice. She then returned to the dinner scene—her mother calling her sorry and her father jumping all over them because he wanted a nice family dinner, even though he was reading the newspaper at the table. She reread her entry in the light of her Hello Kitty lamp.

"A million years from now, people will read my

feelings," she lamented. "They will discover my hurt."
Who would side with parents who were careless in
what they said and lax in their manners?

Carolina brought out her fancy stationery. It was Miss
Manners who should hear about her family and their
breaches of etiquette. She had written Miss Manners
two weeks before and would write her again, though
Carolina suspected that the sage of etiquette had no time
for girls her age. Still, Carolina had made Miss Manners
her heroine. She pictured Miss Manners behind a desk
reading tearstained letters from those seeking solace
from an uncivil world. Miss Manners's posture was perfect, her hair in place despite the temptation to pull it
out after reading her daily correspondence. Carolina
pictured Miss Manners sniffing the flowers on her desk
as she prepared herself for witty replies.

Carolina suddenly sniffed the air about her. It wasn't
flowers scenting her bedroom. Her nostrils flared like a
horse's and her eyes shifted in their sockets. She turned.
"David, you know it's not polite to come in my room
without knocking."

David was munching something.

"Didn't you eat enough at dinner? What are you
eating?" His food-stained T-shirt, which read RAIDERS
NATION, billowed out as if he was hiding something
there.

"Nothing," he mumbled.

"You are, too!"

"No, I'm not."

When he opened his mouth in a smile, Carolina could make out the head of one of his miniature army men. He clamped his mouth shut so that the head stuck out from his lips. The army man appeared to be suffering a new kind of death.

"That is ugly and dirty."

David giggled and ran from the room. Carolina heard him trip in the carpeted hallway. He returned seconds later, a buildup of tears in his eyes.

"What now?"

"I swallowed him."

Carolina stood up. "The army man?"

When he nodded, tears rolled down his cheeks. A new flush of tears filled the space in the corners of his eyes.

"Can you breathe?"

His nod made a tear slip from his face and spill on the floor.

She grabbed his hand, which she discovered was sticky and disgusting—she could only imagine where it had been—and hauled him into the kitchen, where her mother was painting her fingernails. "David swallowed an army man," she said breathlessly. She had to repeat herself over the noise of the dishwasher.

Her mother stood up. "What?" She grabbed David's mouth, pried it open roughly, and looked in.

"Do you see anything?" Carolina wanted to ask.

But she remained quiet, though she did risk leaning toward David's open mouth and taking a peek herself.

"You kids!" her mother scolded. She bent him over her lap and started pounding him on the back in an attempt to dislodge the army man.

"But I didn't do anything," Carolina wanted to say. Instead, she dared to say, "Mom, I think the army man is in his stomach."

"Carlos!" Her mother called Carolina's father. "Carrrrrlooooos." She continued to pat David on the back. She stopped. "Look at my nails. You kids! ¡Cómo friegan!"

Carolina judged that it was time to leave the kitchen. She returned to her bedroom and covered her ears when her parents began to argue—her mother yelled that it was her father's fault for buying army men in the first place. He argued, "My fault? My fault? You're the one always going shopping." Carolina couldn't understand either one's logic and reacted with a disgusted look when the two finally calmed down and her mother suggested they check David's stools for the army man. It would have to come out soon.

Sorry. Her mother said that she was a sorry person, and Carolina didn't know how to respond in a dignified manner. With her little brother in tow, she hurried to school, but not before depositing her letter to Miss Manners in the corner mailbox.

"What did you put in there?" David asked. He was already eating part of his lunch. His fingers and his teeth were orange from Cheetos.

"None of your business."

"I'm going to tell."

"Tell what?" she snapped.

"Tell you put a bomb in there."

Carolina prodded him along. She muttered, "I wish I was from another family." She didn't feel guilty admitting that her loyalty lay elsewhere—who wanted to share a life with a mother who was angry all the time, and a father who spent his evenings tallying box scores of baseball? And she certainly deserved a better brother than one who gobbled army men like candy.

A sixth grader, Carolina still ventured out to the playground—though she had given up tetherball when she got smacked on the nose. Even her interest in kickball, her favorite noontime sport, waned that year when a boy tripped her rounding second base. Her recess was given over to playing catch with her friend Elena, the two of them openmouthed in semiterror as the softball floated skyward and quickly descended. They would play awhile and then sit on the bench and talk, their knees pressed together in a polite grown-up manner.

But that morning their relationship changed.

"Elena!" Carolina called, but not too loudly. She raced to see her friend but slowed when she saw that Elena was sitting with a boy. The boy was the lout who had tripped her the year before and called her clumsy, among other things, after she told her teacher on him. She wondered what Miss Manners would do at such a moment, which worsened when Carolina noticed that Elena had nudged herself closer to the boy.

Disgusting. Carolina brooded. Still, she approached the two and greeted them brightly with, "Good morning." She stood in front of them and eyed Elena and then the boy as she waited for an introduction. When it didn't come, she volunteered, "My name is Carolina."

The boy laughed.

Carolina smiled.

The boy laughed harder.

Still, Carolina continued. "And what's your name?"

The boy laughed and said, "You're such a nerd."

Elena lowered her face and chuckled.

Carolina's face reddened and the machinery behind the eyes that produced tears began to start up. "That is not very polite." She was most hurt that her best friend would laugh at her. "Elena, why are you doing this to me?"

Elena hid her laughter in the sleeve of her sweater.

The boy hee-hawed like a donkey, and Carolina seized the notion that he had in fact a donkey's brain in what she felt was an unshapely skull. Thus, she reasoned, he should be pitied, because in the end, in adulthood, he would be working at a donkey's job.

But as for Elena, one of the smartest girls in class,

Carolina could find no excuse for such poor behavior, poor form. Then she realized their friendship had ended—gone were the times when they played in Elena's tree house, took swimming lessons together, dressed up for Halloween. She knew for sure when Elena took the boy's hand into hers.

"Excuse me," Carolina said before the tears surfaced. She picked up her backpack and left to write Miss Manners on the stationery she always carried to school. "What should you do when you discover a friend is no longer a friend?" she composed on her Hello Kitty stationery. She wrote in purple ink, though she felt the question she posed really required storm-cloud black. She wiped away tears and through the blur of a crushing hurt could see how people—even best friends—could be cruel. She finished her letter, unpeeled a stamp, lined it up correctly on the envelope, and gave the letter to the school secretary, who promised that it would go out in the afternoon mail.

That day Carolina ate alone, a napkin in her lap as she nibbled her sandwich—tuna with a pickle and sheet of lettuce. She wished her mother had cut it into halves. Sandwiches looked better when cut, more sophisticated and delicate.

"When I grow up, I'll cut all my sandwiches into quarters." She picked up the sandwich and ate carefully. She enjoyed the crunchy sound of her carrot sticks and wiped the corners of her mouth when she was through. With nowhere to go, with no one to talk to, she sat on the bench. From there she watched two boys filling their mouths with water from the drinking fountain. They would fill up and then chase each other around, spurting water on each other. They laughed.

"You ugly frog!" one boy called. He was wiping water from his eyes.

Carolina bristled when she discovered the voice belonged to her little brother, David. "The brat," she muttered.

When David cupped a hand into his armpit and began to produce flatulent sounds, she was inclined to get up and make him stop. Instead she deposited her lunch bag in the garbage can and went into the library. There she did some of her work and thumbed through a *National Geographic* magazine, stopping to size up Shetland ponies. *They're so cute,* she thought, and ran a finger down their manes. How she wanted to pet that pony and whisper in its ears, "You're beautiful." She wanted to mount the pony and ride it through the green fields to a river. She could free herself from school and . . . family. She turned the page of the magazine to discover Queen Elizabeth staring at her. The ponies, the article said, belonged to the queen and were pastured at Windsor Castle. Carolina appraised the photograph and noticed the queen's posture. It was straight, dignified, and—*That's it!*—royal.

"I wouldn't mind being a pony," Carolina confessed at last, "as long as I got to live at the castle." She imagined herself eating an apple from the queen's outstretched and gloved hand.

When the bell rang, she stood up and pushed the chair in. That's what the queen would have done—pushed the chair in even though she was royalty. Things, after all, had to be in their rightful place. She felt happy, but within a few steps her spirit sagged. Elena was walking with her hand around that nasty boy's arm. Carolina slowed to a halt. She let them move ahead of her and disappear into the hordes of students. She then felt a nudge when someone clipped her with a backpack.

"Watch where you're going, stupid!" the boy snarled.

Carolina ignored the boy and other bully types knocking her with their backpacks. Her mind was spinning into a dark hole where creepy dreams brewed their sticky liquids. She understood that the relationship between Elena and her had really changed, that she was on her own, alone. Then she heard the word *Sorry* rise above the students running toward their classrooms. "Sorry!" someone yelled, but it could have been, "You're sorry."

David tightened his fists.

"Come on!" Carolina scolded. "Let me see!"

He unfurled his hands and turned them over, revealing palms with rivers of dark, grimy lines.

"I knew it," Carolina remarked. "I knew they would be dirty. You're disgusting."

"So?" David replied. He sucked the mucus in his nostrils and swallowed.

"You're going to get sick," she warned him. "And blow your nose!"

"I'm already sick." He wiped his nose against his sleeve.

"And I saw you spitting water at that kid today."

"But he spit water at me first." He inhaled his mucus again. "It was fun."

Carolina exhaled in frustration that her little brother was a lost cause. She went to her bedroom to write in her diary about Elena. *Why,* she wrote, *why would a friend since first grade laugh at me? And sit so close to that boy!!!* She let her emotions flow on the unlined pages of her diary and was feeling better when the phone rang. She rose, remembering to scoot her chair against her desk, and screamed, "I got it!" Then she fumed at herself. "Don't scream. It's not polite." She also winced at the words *"I got it."* The phrase was barbaric. She hurried to the telephone in the hallway and answered the phone on the fourth ring, "Hello, the Garcias' residence."

"Hi," a boy's dull voice mumbled.

"Who is this?"

"Me."

Carolina could make out giggling in the background. The giggling belonged to Elena, her ex-friend, the subject of today's diary entry. She figured that the two had gone to Elena's house to make this prank call.

"Please don't call again," Carolina said coolly, and lowered the phone, done with Elena for good but not before the two pranksters shouted "Nerd!" in her ear. She walked slowly away and sat on the couch. After a moment tears filled her eyes. She buried her face in her sleeve.

"Why are they so mean?" she blubbered. She figured she would devote the time after dinner to answering that question in her diary.

"Who's mean?" David asked.

She looked up.

"Go away!" She wiped away her tears with her sleeve and buried her face again.

David stood watching his big sister cry. Then he said proudly, "It came out."

"What?" she asked, her shoulders heaving, but not looking up.

"The army man."

At first Carolina didn't understand his meaning. Then she remembered the army man from the night before. She pictured her brother on the toilet and his face pleated from a long, painful strain. "Ah, you're gross!" She got up from the couch and stomped to her bedroom. She put on her coat and left the house, mindful of the time—four-fifteen. Their mother would be home from work soon, and their father, a carpenter, possibly even earlier, or maybe not at all.

Carolina was expected to take care of David and see that he stayed out of trouble, which meant out of the refrigerator—her mother was scared that he was "turning into a little pig"—to use her words. Still, she left her brother alone and stood first on the porch and then sat on the greenest part of their lawn. She watched a truck roll slowly past, its speakers pumped loud and throwing out rap that she—maybe others, too—couldn't understand. Words or no words, the sounds were threatening.

Then she rose as she saw the mail carrier crossing the street, his leather sack on his shoulder nearly empty because theirs was the last block on his route. The mail carrier was Herman Gonzalez, who had won a million dollars in the California lottery. His smiling face appeared in English- and Spanish-language newspapers, plus a Chinese-language newspaper, she had heard. When he was asked by a reporter if he would quit his job, he said, "No, I like my work." Carolina, then ten, had to wonder if he did, or if he just wanted more money. But the mail carrier was forced to take off work for six months because desperate people, even thugs, began to follow him on his delivery route. They would ask—beg with their hands out—for some of his million dollars. He would smile, laugh it off, and say that he wasn't Herman Gonzalez the millionaire but Henry Gonzalez the mail carrier with flat feet. But he was a bad actor, and they followed him until the police escorted him for a day and then advised him to take time off or perhaps work at a desk job for the postal service.

"Hey, little one," the mail carrier sang. He handed her their mail and hurried away as if she were going to ask for some of his million.

She looked through the mail and nearly jumped when she fingered among the bills a letter from Miss Manners.

"Oh my," Carolina chirped. She sat on the front porch, mindful of her posture and that a special moment was upon her, one that might never occur again. She carefully opened the letter. With her hands shaking, she read: *Because of the many letters she receives, Miss Manners is unable to respond to you personally. She regrets that she cannot reply to your problem but suggests that you seek advice from your parent(s), special aunt or uncle, pastor or rabbi, or older person whom you trust. She wishes you well.*

It was signed, *Personal Assistant to Miss Manners.*

"Personal assistant to Miss Manners," Carolina remarked dreamily. She reread the letter—the note, really—and wondered what a personal assistant did. She imagined this person opening the door for Miss Manners. She imagined the personal assistant plucking wilted roses from the vase on the desk where Miss Manners wrote her advice. Maybe she addressed the letters and pressed the stamps in the corner—*I can do that!* Carolina told herself. *I'm sure I can!*

Carolina would have conjured up other tasks for the personal assistant, but her father's truck squeaked up the driveway. Her mother was in the cab and sitting far from her father. Her look was the look of dark clouds and thunder.

"I told you the car was no good!" her mother yelled as she got out and slammed the door.

"You told me a lot of things!" her father fired back.

"What does that mean?" She stopped and propped her hands on her hips. "What does that mean, you dropout!"

Her father had no answer.

Carolina was quick in picking up the conversation. Her father had bought a car from a friend and the car, it seemed, had broken down. But Carolina wasn't quick to get out of their way as they stomped up the porch. Her mother pushed her aside without a greeting and her father stepped over her as if she were a hurdle. They went inside arguing, the screen door slamming behind them.

Carolina got up, crying, "Darn!" Her mother's angry footwork up the porch steps had torn a hole in Miss Manners's letter. Carolina smoothed the letter and almost cursed, but she was aware that Miss Manners would not approve. She turned and spied through the front window her mother making stabbing motions at her father. Her father was waving his hands around as if he were drowning. Her brother was on the couch, swigging from the liter bottle of Dr Pepper and watching the scene between husband and wife. It was all sick, and Carolina nearly became sick in the rosebushes that stood scraggly in front of the porch.

"Help me, Miss Manners," she whispered as she walked down the street. "Help me; help me grow up and get away." *Yes*, Carolina thought. *I'll grow up real pretty and smart and become Miss Manners's personal assistant. I'll open doors for her; open some letters, too.* Carolina bit a fingernail as she wondered if Miss Manners would really hire her. *Yes, she will*, she concluded. *I have manners; I have dreams; I'll change the flowers on the desk for you.* She saw herself opening a letter not unlike the ones she had sent and personally answering it. She would help someone far away, and that person would grow up to be pretty and smart, too.

Carolina wandered her neighborhood in search of something. In fact, her attention was drawn to houses, parked cars, cats on porches, dogs behind fences, balls on roofs, and even Christmas tree lights still hanging from eaves in April. She couldn't stop her desperate search and had to admit that she was seeking some sign of Miss Manners. She believed she found it when she stopped at one house and narrowed her eyes.

"Oh," she squeaked.

She crossed the street toward what looked like the prettiest flower she had ever seen, something that she wished she could pluck and place in a vase as a surprise on Miss Manners's desk. But as she got closer she discovered that the exotic flower was no flower but a red soda can someone had tossed in the bush. Her soul sagged for the second time in one day. Did beauty and manners really exist?

"Help me," Carolina nearly sobbed as she stepped backward and clutched Miss Manners's letter. The world, she realized, was a sad place when from a few feet away trash could fool someone who walked in beauty.

Yeah, Right

One day Javier Mendoza rode his bike by his aunt Marta's house and saw that she was holding a yard sale on her front lawn. He circled in front of her house, his face hidden in a 49ers football helmet he had found earlier in the alley. His aunt had rigged clothes on a line and had run an extension cord to the yard. A television was turned up loudly and roaring with the sounds of a NASCAR race. On a blanket lay shoes, kitchen utensils, toys, a lamp, and other stuff from closets.

Javier pulled to a halt.

"Hi, *Tía,*" he said as he tugged off his helmet. He was glad to get it off; it smelled. It was heavy, just like a real professional one. But he was too smart to believe that he would be so lucky as to find such a relic in an alley. He was nobody's fool.

It took his aunt a while to recognize her nephew. "Oh, honey, it's you. I'm glad you're here." She was wearing pink slippers and a robe. A huge roller crowned her hair. She looked like she was going to bed.

His aunt had Javier move some boxes from the garage to the front yard, plus climb the roof to turn on the water valve to her cooler. It was April in Fresno and spring break for kids. With the days heating up, kids were already running through sprinklers. Boys his age, thirteen, were going shirtless. That is, if they had strong bodies.

By the time Javier was done with his chores, he was sweaty. His own T-shirt, with BART SIMPSON printed on the front, had come off and then back on when he recognized a girl from school. He had forgotten her name, though he remembered her from his third-grade class. Every week during show-and-tell, she would bring weird stuff. One time she brought penguin eggs, though to him they looked like the eggs his mother had cracked open for morning burritos. Another time she brought a lightbulb she said Thomas Edison had used in an experiment. True, the lightbulb looked old, but come on!

"Hi, Javier," the girl sang sweetly. Her greeting carried the scent of watermelon Jolly Ranchers.

"Hi," Javier said as he lowered his head and tried to recall her name.

"Veronica," she helped out. "Do you live here?"

"Nah, my aunt does." Javier turned and saw that his aunt was smiling at him. She lifted her eyelids as she appraised Veronica. Javier picked up the message. His aunt was thinking the girl, Veronica, looked cute. But she wouldn't think that if she had been there in third grade watching Veronica brag during show-and-tell. Right then Javier remembered her bringing in a baseball hit by Sammy Sosa. The baseball looked too new, Javier insisted at the time. There were no dents or scuffs. Javier argued that if Sammy Sosa connected on that ball, the entire cover would be ripped off. Plus, how did she get the ball anyhow?

"You need any more help?" Javier asked.

"No, *mi'jo.*"

His aunt viewed her yard sale. To Javier it looked like a tornado had ripped through the house and scattered her belongings. "Would you like a soda?" she said as she turned to face Javier and Veronica.

"I guess so," Javier shrugged.

"And you?" She was looking at Veronica, who was holding up a half-dressed Ken doll.

Veronica set down Ken, but not before saying that she had twenty Kens lined up on a bedroom shelf and that one day she would sell them when they were worth a lot of money. Her twenty Barbies were in a hope chest.

Javier didn't care enough to ask what a hope chest was, though to him it sounded like it could be a workout station where you build up your muscles.

"Thank you," Veronica said. Her face brightened

into a smile. Her tongue was red from the watermelon Jolly Ranchers. "I would love one—any kind." She then volunteered that she had helped her mother wash the car. She added in a near whisper that Ferraris are really hard to clean because of all the chrome.

Javier rocked on his heels—what a liar!

"That's nice," Aunt Marta said in an encouraging tone.

"Plus, I did some of the ironing because our nanny quit. She had to go back to France because of a family thing."

"Yeah, right," Javier grumbled to himself.

"That's real nice," his aunt said from the porch before she disappeared into the house.

Veronica stepped toward the snowy television. There was a wreck on the track, and the race cars were moving slowly past a man waving a red flag. "I'm going to get my driver's license when I'm fifteen."

Javier was immediately pulled into the debate. "You can't do that," he argued.

"Yeah, you can. I'm going to New Mexico to get my license. That's where my dad lives. He says you can get a driver's license when you're fifteen."

Javier bit the inside of his tongue as he almost cried out, *Liar.*

"My dad has a farm there. He said that we can race tractors if we want. He has three of them. On the farm he has room to land his plane."

"No way," Javier blurted. He slapped his hand over his mouth and through his fingers uttered a muffled "Sorry." He didn't wish to be rude.

"Yeah, it's true. His farm is really big. It would be bigger except he had to sell some of it because someone wanted to drill an oil well on it."

Javier wished she would go away. But he let her talk as she described the kind of car she was going to get—a convertible Audi TT. He let her babble as his interest grew in the racetrack wreck and the driver they were pulling out of the race car. His head hung limply. *Is he alive?* Javier wondered.

Aunt Marta came out of the house. She was no longer wearing her robe, slippers, or curler as she had prepared herself for the day as a merchant. She wore a sweater with an Easter bunny stitched on the front. Its tail was a fuzzy pom-pom.

"Thank you," Veronica said when she took the root beer from his aunt. "Root beer is my favorite. In fact, I used to make root beer at home."

"Oh, how nice," Aunt Marta remarked lightly.

"It's really easy, except when you try to get the fizz to stay." Veronica took a sip. "You need really good corks. Plus the bottles can't be too big. The fizz goes out of them if they are."

Javier took a long swig and then—he couldn't help himself—burped.

Aunt Marta frowned at Javier.

"My dad lives in New Mexico," Veronica continued. "He used to make root beer, but now he farms onions. I like onion rings with mustard. I know it's weird, but I like 'em that way." She went on to say that her father had a helicopter that he used to patrol his ranch, which was different from the farm. The ranch had cattle and some wild mustangs. She said that he would use his jet, except that it went too fast to count his herds.

Aunt Marta's smile weakened.

Javier swiveled away from the last big fat lie. He grimaced as he wished that he could jump into the television and do something useful, like help the hurt race car driver. When Veronica began to explain the three tractors—the two that ran, the one rusting by the barn where they kept root beer bottles just in case—Javier excused himself and went inside. He said he had to go to the restroom and hurried up the steps as if he really had to go.

"Don't let Chalupa out!" Aunt Marta yelled. Chalupa was her Chihuahua, a spoiled dog that wore a tiny raincoat on cold days. On really cold days, when ice blanketed the lawn, his aunt attached a hand warmer inside the raincoat. Javier had yet to figure out why the dog never started smoking and caught on fire.

From inside, Javier peered out the front window.

"Dang!" he yelled. "What is she doing here?" He punched a pillow.

Chalupa rounded the corner from the kitchen. He was dressed in a pink sweater.

"Hey, dog," Javier said by way of greeting as he wiggled his fingers at Chalupa. But Chalupa, rolling up his tongue that disappeared into his mouth, wouldn't come. "Forget you, then!"

Javier waited for Veronica to leave. But she remained on the front lawn, picking among the yard-sale items, and finally left only after Javier really had to go to the bathroom. When he returned from the bathroom and peered out the front window, where Chalupa had left his nose print, he squeezed his hands into fists and cheered, "Great!" He went outside. His grumbling aunt wouldn't look directly at him. Then she asked, "How do you know that girl?"

"I don't know her," Javier argued.

"She said you do. She just talks and talks."

"*Tía*, really—I don't know her! Why do you think I went inside?"

"Did you jiggle the handle on the toilet? It'll run if you don't." She picked at the pom-pom absently. "*Pues*, at least she bought something."

Javier scanned the things on the front lawn. "What did she buy?"

"The helmet."

"The football helmet! It was mine!" He stabbed a finger at his chest.

"I didn't know that," Aunt Marta explained innocently. "It was on the lawn, *qué no?*" She licked her lips as she searched for an excuse. "She bought it for three dollars. How 'bout if I get to keep just a dollar for me?"

When Javier got home, his mother screamed from the kitchen that he had gotten a phone call.

"Who was it?" Javier asked as he went into the kitchen.

His mother was seated at the kitchen table. Her elbows were propped in lemon halves. His mother believed that the acid helped dissolve the discolored skin on her elbows. Javier had tried that process, too, but all he got was sticky elbows. And Javier was suspicious of his mother's other home remedies. Sometimes she would rest on the couch with slices of cucumber over her eyes. If she had a headache, she would place cool sheets of lettuce on her forehead.

"I don't know," she answered. She turned a page of *National Enquirer* magazine. His mother was reading an article about an obese woman who lived on tomato juice for two weeks. By the end of that time, she could slip back into the bikini she wore in high school. As proof, there were "before" and "after" pictures.

Javier got himself a glass of water. He sat down with his mother and they read the article together— that one and one about a man who fell from a plane and lived to tell his story.

"See," his mother said.

Javier was about to ask, "See what?" when the cordless telephone on the kitchen counter rang. He picked up, and before he could say hello, a girl on the other end related in a rapid-fire voice, "Your football helmet, the one I bought, used to belong to Jeff Garcia."

It was Veronica. He hurried from the kitchen.

"I bet it's worth about three hundred dollars," Veronica said. "Maybe more."

Although he knew who was on the line, he asked, "Who's this?" He pictured her in a frilly bedroom where a wall was lined with those Kens she had spoken about.

"It's me, silly—Veronica." Veronica said she had placed the helmet on sale on eBay and that if she sold it, she'd give him half of the money.

Javier's tongue couldn't move. He presumed the football helmet was just some thing that some old jock had thrown away. But an authentic 49ers helmet worn by Jeff Garcia! His tongue finally moved. "How do you know it's really real?"

"His signature. It's on the inside of the helmet."

"But it could be a fake."

"No, I don't think so," she sang. She explained that she had looked up his signature on the Internet, and his looping script matched the name inside the helmet.

Javier's tongue died again. He didn't know how to respond when she said she had sold a lot of things on eBay. If he wanted, he could look under "charming-girl," the account she and her father shared.

"The onion farmer with a helicopter?" asked Javier snidely.

Veronica chuckled. "That's right. But let's not forget the cattle and horses he owns. Plus the vineyard in Napa. My dad is flying in to see me this weekend."

Javier fumed. He hung up as she was asking if she could call him later. He returned to the kitchen to read the *National Enquirer*. He and his mother read about a sixty-nine-year-old grandmother who had entered a bodybuilding contest and took second place.

"Wow!" Javier said, impressed.

But Javier's mother noticed the grandmother's dark elbows. What she needed was a single hour of her elbows set in lemon halves in order to come out as top dog.

Javier got it into his head that he could hold a yard sale. True, it wasn't eBay, but with a week off for spring break, he had to do something. He looked under his bed and in the garage for stuff to sell. He brought out to the yard old clothes, a Monopoly game, a broken Nintendo, a tricycle, a tarnished teapot, and his army men. He also set out a computer and a plastic guitar his father had given him. Javier posted a sign on the telephone pole on the corner. The sign read: YARD SAIL.

He sat in a chair and waited for the hordes. When

no one came except his cat, sniffing each and every sale item, he set up the Monopoly set and played against himself. He chose the iron as his marker and played against the horse. He was mad when the horse began to pile up all the hotels and five-hundred-dollar bills. The iron was luckless.

"Dang," Javier moaned when he landed on Park Place and had to pay up a thousand dollars he didn't have. He considered cheating. There was no one around to see him steal the horse's five-hundred-dollar bills. Instead, he swiped his hand over the hotels, ending the game. Javier sighed as he lay back, hands behind his head. His head immediately heated up. The shade had moved and then he found himself—and all his yard-sale stuff—sitting in direct sun. As he got up to move his stuff, he heard someone call, "Javier, look at this."

Javier turned and saw Veronica coming up the sidewalk on a dirt bike. She skidded to a halt, her ponytail whipping about her face.

Javier approached Veronica. "What?"

"Guess!"

Javier didn't like the game.

"I don't wanna guess."

Veronica begged him by pouting and stomping her foot. "Please, pretty pleeeease!"

Javier didn't like the "pretty please" stuff. What did she mean with that? It struck him that maybe she was flirting. The only thing he liked about her at that moment was her dirt bike. He was envious of her ride, while his own bike had been put together by an uncle who had stolen most of the parts.

"Veronica, I don't understand you."

Veronica smiled. "That's cute! That's the first time you called me Veronica. Do you know what that means?"

Javier was clueless.

"It means—" Veronica stopped. She said that she would e-mail him what it meant.

He lied and said that he didn't have e-mail.

"You got to get with it, then," she sang.

Stupid me, Javier thought. *If I hadn't put this stuff out for a yard sale, she wouldn't have ever shown up.* She was a pest, or worse, a pest who thought they were friends. But suddenly his tune changed when Veronica pulled out some hundred-dollar bills. His nostrils flared at the sight of those bills; yes, they smelled like real money, not like the Monopoly money on the lawn.

"I sold the Jeff Garcia helmet on eBay." She reminded him that her account was "charminggirl."

"No way," he remarked after she had stopped jabbering. "You sold it?"

"Yeah, and the buyer lives right in town. He drove over this morning and paid in cash. He loves the 49ers. He went to college in San Francisco—that's why."

But what does this mean for me? Javier wondered.

"And I love . . ." Veronica's eyes became shiny. She moved her bike a few inches closer to Javier. The front tire touched his knee.

Oh god, no, Javier thought as he took a step back. *She likes me.*

"And I would love to give you fifty-fifty. Like two hundred and fifty dollars." She said that it was really his helmet, and she couldn't possibly live with herself if she kept all the money. She handed Javier two one-hundred-dollar bills and said that they would have to cash the last bill to make it fair.

"No, th-that's okay," Javier stuttered. He was glad to slip the two hundred dollars into his front pocket. His eyes fell on the stuff on the lawn and the Monop-oly money that began to blow away. His belongings looked pathetic, like stuff that falls from the back of a pickup truck on the freeway.

"Oh, that's pretty," Veronica said of the tarnished teapot. "How much is it?"

That piece of junk, Javier thought. It had been in the garage for years and years, or since he was a kid when he first made mud cakes in the backyard. He had used the teapot to mix mud. It was nothing to him. His in-stinct was to give it away, but he remembered the foot-ball helmet. Perhaps the teapot was worth something. "How about thirty dollars?" he braved.

Veronica opened and closed the top of the teapot and rubbed it like a magic lamp. She agreed to the price, which made Javier wonder if he should have charged more.

"But I need to break this hundred," she said, snapping the bill between her fingers. "I need to pay you fifty, plus thirty for the teapot." Her eyes twinkled. "How 'bout I let you keep all of the hundred if you . . . god, I'm shameless." She waved a hand in front of her reddening face and completed her sentence. "You can keep it all if you take me out for a smoothie."

Javier swallowed as he did his math. He figured that he would have to treat her to a smoothie, and what would that cost but two dollars? But he was aware that he was walking on eggshells—he looked down at his feet—no, Monopoly money. He was smothering a pile of twenty-dollar bills.

"Come on," Veronica pleaded.

He nearly grimaced at the thought of listening to an hour or so of lies about her mother's Ferrari and her dad's farm and helicopter and stuff. Still, he felt it was a business call. He took a step, and a twenty-dollar bill of Monopoly money stuck to the bottom of his shoe. He shook the bill from his sole and coolly accepted the hundred dollars from Veronica.

"Where do you wanna go?"

They rode their bikes down to the Ice Cream Palace, where Javier had a hard time breaking the hundred-dollar bill. The pimply high school student behind the counter complained that he didn't have any change and that the only way he could break the bill was if Javier bought a twenty-dollar gift certificate. Javier considered the proposition. He remembered his mother's birthday was coming up. He could get a certificate for her and—he felt a little ashamed as he licked his lips—was aware that she probably would take him along to the Ice Cream Palace. He would get some of his money back in ice cream.

"Okay," Javier agreed.

The counter boy fixed their order in minutes. They sat on tall stools by the window so that they could watch their bikes. Veronica giggled for no reason and swung her legs.

"It's a beautiful day," Veronica remarked.

For moneymaking, Javier thought. He couldn't wait to get home to examine closely those two hundred-dollar bills in his pocket.

"What do you think of my toes?" She wiggled her blue-painted toenails at Javier.

"They look clean," he answered.

She laughed.

Javier wished she would be quiet and let him suck down his pineapple milkshake—he had changed his mind about a smoothie. He was thinking of stuffing her mouth with napkins when she asked if he wanted to go to a dance with her.

A mouthful of milkshake went down his throat like

vegetables. "I don't know how to dance," he admitted. He sighed.

"Silly, you don't have to know how to dance to go to a dance."

Javier blinked, confused.

"A dance is where you go, you know, to see people, to be with your friends." She sucked some of her strawberry milkshake and then said dreamily, "Like last year in San Francisco. My dad took me there to a sort of pre-coming-out dance. You know what a debutante is?"

Javier shook his head.

"It's like when you turn sixteen and you meet society."

Society, Javier wondered. "What's society?"

"It's like when parents show off what kind of daughter they raised." She described the fancy dance ball she went to in San Francisco. There was an orchestra and waiters in tuxedos and all kinds of food. "I wore long gloves," she said, wiggling her fingers and laughing.

Javier wondered if that dance had been outside. He had heard San Francisco was cold. He asked if it had been cold at the dance.

"No, silly. Everyone wears gloves. White ones."

"The boys, too?"

She nodded her head. Then she pulled a necklace from under her sweatshirt and said, "A boy gave this to me."

Javier sucked a cheekful of milkshake, swallowed, and muttered, "Cool."

"It's a ruby," Veronica whispered, her head leaning between the two milkshakes. "He was really nice. He's in Junior ROTC and is a captain. His dad's a colonel in the air force." She sipped her drink. "My dad used to be a colonel, too. He retired a long time ago, just after my parents broke up."

"That's when he started his onion farm, huh?" Javier could sense a nastiness grow in himself. He didn't believe a word she was saying.

"No, the onion farm was in our family for a really long time. Since the conquistadors came—or something like that." She explained that the Spanish adventurers settled in New Mexico and her family was part of the first settlers. "Of course, we didn't grow onions back then. It was just for sheep, I think." She stirred her drink with a straw. "I'm not really Mexican, like you. I'm Spanish."

Javier gazed out the window at his bicycle. *Just a few more sips of this milkshake,* he reasoned, *and I'm outta here.* He was mad that she was denying she was Mexican. *She's embarrassed,* he growled in his thoughts.

"You know the explorer Cortez? My last name is Cortez. We're related."

"Yeah, right," Javier snarled. "Veronica, you're a liar!"

Veronica's smile disappeared. She let go of her straw, which began to sink into her milkshake.

Immediately, Javier felt bad. "Well, maybe not a liar, but you're making all this up." He couldn't see the difference being lying and making something up, but the latter seemed less offensive.

"I'm not a liar."

"So, your dad has a farm in New Mexico and some grapes in—" He stalled as he tried to remember the place.

"Napa. And yes, he does. He grows zinfandel varietals."

"And he flies a helicopter! And he was a captain in the air force!"

"Colonel," she corrected coolly. She lifted her straw from her milkshake.

Javier's face reddened with anger. He continued in spite of himself: "And you're Spanish, not Mexican like me. And you went to this stupid fancy ball. And you've got all those Barbies and Kens. Plus, your mama drives a Ferrari." His voice had grown louder until he sensed the pimply guy behind the counter sneering at him. Suddenly he lowered his head. *I'm a jerk,* he thought. *I should just let her lie and lie.*

"You know, you're being really awful, Javier." Her voice was about to crack.

The two became silent.

"I'm sorry," he heard himself mutter. He considered plunging his hand into his pocket and giving back her two hundred dollars. Indeed, his hand went into his pocket, felt the crisp texture of new money, but then he brought his hand out empty. He really felt like a jerk when Veronica's eyes filled with tears. When the tears began to spill, he apologized, "I'm sorry. I believe you."

"No, you don't."

"Yeah, I do." He almost crossed his chest and said, "Scout's honor."

Veronica wiped her face, jumped from the stool, and left the store, riding away with the teapot clanging like a bell on the handlebars.

The next day Javier looked up "charminggirl" on eBay.

"Dang," he muttered when he found her account and discovered that she had already posted the teapot for sale. The teapot's price was two hundred dollars, but it was going for over three hundred. Javier looked up from the computer screen. Even though he was full from breakfast—*chorizo con huevos* and *papas* with homemade tortillas—he had an empty feeling in his stomach. He felt that he had lost something precious.

"I'll call her," he said. But he couldn't remember her last name. He knew she shared the name with an explorer, but which one? He asked his mother, who was on the couch in the living room. Her face was layered with lettuce—she was suffering a headache from the buzz of the neighbor's leaf blower. Her hands were fitted with rubber gloves—his mother made her own moisturizer from honey, and she wore gloves to keep it off her clothes and furniture.

"Mom, who's the Spanish explorer?"

"Christopher Columbus."

"He wasn't Spanish."

"Thomas Edison." She held the lettuce on her face as she started to laugh. Her headache, it seemed, was gone.

"Mom, Edison wasn't an explorer!"

"Michael Jackson." She laughed harder.

"No wonder I'm getting Cs in school!"

Javier stomped from the living room as she uttered, "Placido Domingo." He went into the kitchen and was about to call the library to ask about the explorer when the telephone rang. It was Veronica.

"I'm sorry about yesterday," Javier said before she could speak. And he was, and was especially sorry because she had the teapot that was going for hundreds.

"I understand how you might not believe me," Veronica nearly sobbed.

"I do," he lied.

"You do?"

"Yeah, totally."

She asked what he was doing later. Her father had

flown his jet from New Mexico and was going to rent a helicopter to view some vineyards outside of town. Her father was thinking about buying them.

She won't stop, Javier thought. *She lies and lies and lies.* But could he be wrong? The idea flashed in his mind.

"I'm playing baseball," he said. "With some friends."

The friends were little kids and the game was with plastic bats and balls. When she asked where, he told her the vacant lot at the corner of his street.

"I know the place," she said. "That's where people sometimes throw garbage."

"Yeah, that's it."

Javier repeated his apology and had to repeat it a third time when she said she couldn't make out what he was saying. She said she had just gotten a cell phone, the kind with a small screen.

Liar! he shouted in his heart.

He was about to ask her about the teapot when she said that she had to go, that her brother was calling from France. *"Ciao,"* she said, "I'll see you later."

Dang! Javier groaned as he hung up. He had been stupid to trade the teapot. He got back on the computer and searched eBay. It was going for over four hundred dollars.

"It's not fair!" he cried in anger. For a moment he wondered if he was wrong. Maybe she was rich. After all, she did wear nice clothes and he had heard she sometimes had parties at her house. He did remember her buying ice creams for all the girls in third grade. Plus, didn't she seem to pull out hundred-dollar bills from her pocket whenever she wanted? In the end, though, he figured she couldn't be that rich. "No way," he told himself. "She's just like me—like the rest of us."

Javier left the house just as his mother was mixing a bowl of egg whites, a concoction she would apply to her throat. The mixture, she said, would keep her throat from sagging.

"I'll be back," Javier hollered.

He went into the garage to see if there was something worth anything. He kicked among the boxes. He scanned the shelf where his mother kept the detergent and bleach—nothing. He rifled through a laundry basket of old clothes; the sour smell nearly brought tears to his eyes. He wrestled a lawn mower and car parts out of the way to get to a chest of drawers. "It's got to have something," he told himself. When he opened the top drawer, a mouse leaped up and scampered over his shoulder.

"Ahhh!" he screamed.

He hurried out of the garage and seconds later returned to retrieve the plastic bat and balls. Late for the baseball game, he ran to the vacant lot and found the little kids sword fighting with branches.

"You're going to hurt yourselves," Javier said.

"We're already hurt," one kid said. He showed him

the skinned elbow from when he had fallen. Another kid showed him where he had been whacked on the back of his hand.

"Man, you guys," Javier snarled. "Your parents are going to blame me."

"No, they won't," one chubby kid claimed. "They won't care unless we die. That's what they said."

Because he was thirteen and they were only eight-year-olds, Javier played himself against them. But he couldn't concentrate. The image of the teapot kept floating behind the back of his eyes. He imagined it on eBay and its auction price rising to over a thousand dollars.

"She's such a liar," he found himself saying as he swung through a pitch. "Yeah, right, your brother lives in France and you've got a cell phone." He swung and missed again. "Yeah, right, you have the lightbulb that once belonged to Thomas Edison." He swung and missed badly.

He was out, but none of the kids in dirty T-shirts cared. An ice-cream truck rolled up the street and the kids ran after it. Javier was glad they were gone. He sat in the shade of a pomegranate tree and stuck a blade of grass in his mouth. He placed his hand over his brow, as if he were saluting, and made out his cat walking on a neighbor's car.

"You're going to get busted, buster!" he yelled. He

liked his cat because he was an adventurer that sometimes scratched at the front door with a mouse in his
mouth. Javier was about to get up to get him when
the dirt at his feet began to swirl. He heard a sound
above—*whump, whump, whump*—and when he peered
up, in a confused state, thought he was seeing a washing machine falling out of the sky.

His pants began to waver and his T-shirt flapped about
his belly. The dirt powdered his face like makeup.

"Hello down there!" a voice blared through a bullhorn.

It's a helicopter, he realized.

"Did you win?" the voice called.

Veronica, he thought, rubbing his eyes with his fists
to get the dust and disbelief from his eyes.

The helicopter hovered over the vacant lot, swirling
dust and bending the limbs of the pomegranate tree.
The plastic bat and balls rolled away.

Wincing, Javier could make out the pilot—a man
wearing sunglasses and a soldier's hat with a shiny colonel's cluster. He could make out Veronica talking on
a cell phone. She snapped closed the cell phone and
picked up the bullhorn.

"That was my brother. He's flying in to see the
vineyard!" she yelled above the whirl of the helicopter's propellers. "Plus, my dad might buy the lake next
to it." She then dipped her hand into a sack. "Catch!"

Veronica tossed what he believed was a discolored baseball. But when he caught it, he discovered it was an onion. He sniffed it and recalled her saying that her father had an onion farm in New Mexico.

"I'll see you at school!" she yelled.

He had no choice but to wave as the helicopter lifted slowly and banked away, but not before he heard her yell through the bullhorn, "I'm taking off a week to go to Florida—sorry you can't come!"

He watched the helicopter until it was a speck in the sky.

"Yeah, right," he answered with dirt on his tongue and an onion he tossed like a baseball from one hand to the next. "Yeah, right."

How Becky Garza Learned Golf

Becky Garza rubbed an old T-shirt up the shaft of her five wood and marveled how the chrome-plated shaft sparkled in the hot summer light. Uncle Andy had given her a set of used clubs (minus the putter) with the promise to take her to the golf course when she got good. And in order to get good, she figured, she had to practice. She first practiced in her backyard, but her cat, Samba, kept chasing the golf ball. Then she practiced in the living room but had to stop that when the golf ball slammed against the television screen. Becky was spooked. *That was close,* she thought. How would she explain a spiderweb-like crack like that? Her parents didn't like her horsing around in the house.

The solution, she decided, was to make her own golf course in the vacant corner lot. She spent two whole days removing rocks, boards, car parts, bicycle parts, paint cans, and other debris. She raked away litter and cut the long, brittle grass. Some kids from school came by to see what she was doing. They straddled their bikes, spitting sunflower-seed shells, and asked, "What are you doing?" She explained the course, and they listened awhile before riding away doing wheelies.

Becky was in competition with her friend Dulce Rosales. Dulce was a smallish girl who played tough at all sports, especially soccer. Dulce wasn't afraid of playing football with boys or handball with grownups. She tied back her ponytail and taunted, "Let's go." But Becky felt that Dulce was too rough to understand the subtle nature of golf. Golf was a thinking person's sport, Uncle Andy said. Becky wiped her face and complained, "Man, it's hot."

"What's hot is my play, you mean," said Dulce, who was using a three wood as her putter. On her knees, face close to the ground, she had the club positioned between her thumb and index finger and was pretending to shoot pool. With one eye closed, she slid the club back and forth and then struck the golf ball. The ball traveled six feet straight into the hole.

"That's not how you play golf!" Becky exclaimed.

Dulce rose to her feet, her knees powdered brown from the sandy dirt. "The ball went in, didn't it?"

Becky fumed. She didn't know the rules of golf but

didn't believe that using a club like a pool stick was in the books. Still, she didn't say anything more. She felt confident.

"Okay, my turn," Becky said, and lowered her club, eyeing first the golf ball, then the hole. She wiggled her body a little, just like the pros do on television, and then tapped the golf ball. The ball rolled four feet and to the left.

"Too bad, girl!" Dulce cried.

Becky furrowed her brow and bit her lip. She took a second shot and that one stopped an inch short of the hole.

"You got to put a little meat into it!" Dulce sang.

Becky got the ball into the hole on the third putt. She picked up her ball and said, "Dulce, you're not supposed to talk to the other player."

"What other player?" Dulce asked seriously. She looked around.

"The other player is . . . me," Becky said. She swallowed painfully. The score was one to three. *How is that possible?* she wondered.

They studied the second of eighteen holes. It was in a small valley and the ground was cement hard.

"You go first," Becky said.

"Nah, girl," Dulce mumbled. She had a length of red whip licorice hanging from her mouth. She chewed a little and said, "You go first."

"But you're in the lead."

Dulce shrugged. She stood and used the club properly. She took a practice swing, the red whip licorice dangling from her mouth. She swung the club back and smacked the ball, which went racing left and then corrected to the right. The golf ball disappeared into the hole.

Dulce threw the golf club into the air. She pumped her arm and yelled, "I'm hot, man!" She fitted a few inches of red whip into her mouth.

"Dulce," Becky growled, "you're not supposed to be eating in the presence of the other player."

Dulce laughed. "And you're the other player, huh?"

Becky nodded.

Dulce gobbled more of the red whip but first offered Becky a few inches by pulling and breaking it into halves.

"No, thank you," Becky said as she dropped her golf ball and lined up a putt. She measured in her mind the distance between the ball and the hole. She wiggled and adjusted her stance. She then let the club rise and fall, striking the ball past the hole by four feet.

"That's too bad, girl!" Dulce said. "You got to do it a little smoother. Let me show you." Dulce stepped toward Becky, who turned her body away and suddenly had a great interest in the house across the street.

"Don't be like that!" Dulce warned.

"Like what?"

"Like a friend can't teach you. I mean, Tiger had to learn from someone. ¿Qué no?"

Becky glowered at Dulce but was surprised that Tiger Woods was in her vocabulary. She thought, *Yeah, maybe she's right.* Tiger started somewhere and with someone's help. But for the time being, Becky felt she should play by instinct. She approached her golf ball and knelt down, her hands cupped around her eyes as she studied the distance and terrain of the course.

"Whatta you doing?" Dulce asked.

Becky rose quickly and ignored her friend.

"I'm studying the ball," Becky said.

Dulce laughed. "That's funny—studying the ball, like you're in school or something."

Becky mumbled and took her stance. She placed her club behind the golf ball. But while she was adjusting her stance, her club struck the golf ball by mistake.

"Hey, that counts!" Dulce yelled, jabbing a finger at the golf ball. "I saw it."

Becky swung around to her friend. "It was a mistake."

"Yeah, but you hit the ball, didn't you?" She was gobbling a handful of Nerds. The corners of her mouth were stained red from candy.

Becky had to admit that she had struck the golf ball. But it had traveled only two inches. "That wasn't a hit," she argued to herself. Wasn't there a rule about a golf ball touched by mistake? She was about to concede the stroke when Dulce cried, "Okay, I'll let you off this time. But that's it, girl." She then rattled a box of Nerds at Becky. "Want some? They'll give you energy."

Becky refused the candy and refused to give up, though by the ninth hole she was behind twenty-four hits to sixteen by Dulce, who had finished the box of Nerds and was then eating sunflower seeds.

"I oughta go pro," Dulce bragged. She spit out the shells of sunflower seeds. "Except this game is boring." She smacked her lips. "I'm thirsty, too."

"It's not boring," Becky argued.

"When you're in the lead it is." She spanked her golf ball without concentration, and the ball rolled and went into the hole. She let the golf club fall from her grip. "Did you see that?"

Becky's shoulders slumped.

Dulce lifted her face skyward. There was the sound of an approaching vehicle. "It's my *papi.*"

A rattling pickup truck filled with his kids and other kids rounded the corner. The horn tooted.

"There's a fire!" Dulce screamed.

Dulce's father was an amateur ham radio operator. A large antenna was propped up on his roof. His radio was able to pick up police and fire calls. He didn't respond to police calls, but if someone's house was burning, he would yell, "Fire—let's go! *¡Ándale!*" Dulce's father argued that his interest in fire was a community service. It taught kids not to play with matches.

Dulce ran off but turned and said, "You win!" She leaped over every hole she had won, and that was all of them.

But Becky didn't feel like a winner under the hot summer sun. She was disgusted with her play. How did someone loud and rough like Dulce beat her? Wasn't golf supposed to be subtle and a thinking person's sport? She gathered the golf balls and clubs and walked home with her bag on her shoulder.

"Hi, Mom!" she called out. But no one was home, though the cooler was on and stirring the newspaper on the coffee table. The newspaper was opened to the sports section. Tiger Woods was smiling with a trophy hoisted over his head.

Becky went into the kitchen and got herself a glass of grape Kool-Aid. She returned to the living room. She plopped herself down on the couch and zapped on the television. Tiger Woods's face appeared and nearly filled the television screen with his bright, toothy smile. He had just putted a fifteen footer, and the crowd behind him was cheering. Becky looked behind her when she heard a tap on the window. It was her cat, Samba, wanting to come in.

"You can't come in," she told her.

The cat was allowed into the house only when it rained.

Becky zapped off the television, got up, and pulled out a club—a two iron—from her bag. She dropped a golf ball onto the rug and lined up a shot that rolled under the left end of the coffee table. She mumbled, "It was an accident." She was thinking of the third hole when she had carelessly struck the ball on her backswing.

"But it's not going to be an accident if you break the TV?" Becky's mother asked. "Or the window. Or the lamp." Her mother hurried in small steps across the living room with a potted plant in her arms. She set the plant by the window.

Becky picked up the ball.

"Are you hungry?" Becky's mother asked, breathing hard from the exertion of carrying the pot.

"A little bit," Becky answered. She told her mother she had played against Dulce but didn't say she had lost.

Her mother fixed her two bean burritos and went outside. Becky devoured them within minutes and, one by one, licked her fingers. She got up, went into the kitchen, and looked in the refrigerator—she was still hungry. When a hard-boiled egg caught her eye, she couldn't help but think of a golf ball.

"I need to practice," she told herself, and closed the refrigerator. She squeezed on the hard-boiled egg, but it didn't break. She squeezed harder until she felt the shell crack. "I'm going to beat Dulce."

Becky returned to the living room and turned on the television again. Tiger Woods was crouched and studying the line between the putter and the hole. His hands were cupped around his face, which was stern-looking with determination. He stood up, positioned himself next to the ball, wiggled his body, and let his putter guide the ball.

Becky was already asleep by the time the ball traveled left to right and found the hole.

Becky challenged Dulce the next day, and Becky lost sixty-five strokes to fifty-four. She challenged her the following day, and again Becky lost with the embarrassing score of sixty-seven against Dulce's fifty-one. Becky challenged her a third time after she had called Uncle Andy for tips on putting. He kept repeating that the lightness of grip was all-important. He also apologized for not providing her with a putter and promised to get her one for Christmas, if he didn't spot one on sale sooner.

But to Becky's new challenge, Dulce argued, "What's the point, girl? You know the outcome before we even start." Also, Dulce had plans to go swimming. She had a bet against some boy that she could hold her breath underwater longer than he.

Becky went out alone to her homemade golf course at the corner.

"I'm not going to go home until I win," she told herself as she set her bag down. She was going to play against herself. She figured that she had to beat the

course record of fifty-one, a record held—she gulped—
by Dulce. But first she had to clean up a pile of dog
poop that was between holes three and four. She
scooped it up with a board and carried the mess to a
far corner.

Then she approached the first hole. She dropped
the ball and took out a smaller club than she had
used before, a four iron. She gripped it lightly, like her
uncle said, and practiced swinging effortlessly. "Be like
Tiger," she commanded herself. *Like Tiger.* But when
she swung for real, the golf ball moved only a foot.

"Darn it!" she scolded herself.

She took a second shot, and the golf ball skipped
beyond the hole.

"Stupid ball!" she muttered.

She spent the morning in the vacant lot, and with
each round she got worse. She had completed the first
round with sixty strokes and the second round with
sixty-nine, though she argued with herself that it was
really a sixty-eight. Her ball would have gone in, except there was a small wood chip in front of the hole.

Tired, Becky sat in the shade of the fence that sepa-
rated her golf course from a neighbor's yard. She peeked
between the slats of the warped fence. She could see
Doña Carmen Maria sweeping her back steps. In her
hands the broom operated like a golf club—Doña Carmen Maria could manage only small swings that gath-

ered dust and a few leaves from her mulberry tree. She was old.

Becky's mother said their family was related to Doña Carmen Maria. It was through a cousin of a cousin or something like that. The old woman occasionally visited them, shuffling down the street with two sweaters on—she was always complaining about the cold, even in the summer, when the sun yellowed lawns, cracked the ground, and darkened children to the color of mud. Becky hated when Doña Carmen Maria would pinch her cheek and say, *"¡Qué linda chica!"*

Becky's club, which was resting in her lap, accidentally knocked against the fence. Doña Carmen Maria stopped sweeping. Becky could see the old woman's eyes narrow. Her whiskery mouth pinched into a small knot. She took a few rickety steps toward Becky.

"It's me," Becky braved as she stood up. "You know, Becky." She pushed herself up onto the fence and showed her face to Doña Carmen Maria.

"Oh, you," the old woman said. In Spanish, she asked Becky what she was doing.

In English, Becky told the old woman she was playing golf.

Doña Carmen Maria's face brightened. *"Como Tigre Woods, qué no? El joven es magnífico."*

Becky was surprised that she would know Tiger Woods. In her eyes her hero, Tiger, had grown even larger. Why would an old woman like Doña Carmen Maria be aware of a golf legend?

"Yeah, like him," she answered. And to her surprise, Doña Carmen Maria came down her driveway and out of her yard. Queenie, her small dog with crooked teeth, followed. Becky dreaded the cheek-pinching routine but was prepared. She was already wincing when the old woman, smiling a nearly toothless smile, raised a hand and twisted her cheek and said how pretty she was.

Becky fought the urge to wipe her cheek of the old woman's touch.

"¿Cómo estás, mi'ja?" she asked, an ancient finger playing with a mole on her throat. "¿Y tus padres?"

Becky answered that she was okay and her parents were fine. She said her mother was at the beauty parlor.

Doña Carmen Maria shivered. "Hace frío." She adjusted the sweater on her shoulders. She also adjusted Queenie's sweater.

If anything, Becky was burning up. It was two-thirty in the afternoon, the hottest time of the day.

Doña Carmen Maria scanned the vacant lot. She asked if someone was buying the lot because it was clean.

"I cleaned it up," Becky said. "I made it into a golf course."

Doña Carmen Maria smiled. "Like Tiger."

Becky hoisted a small smile that lasted only a few seconds.

Doña Carmen Maria reached for one of the clubs in the bag. She said it was like a sword. She poked the air and laughed to herself.

Becky didn't smile. She was hot, thirsty, and uneasy with the old woman who again started to play with the mole on her throat. But Becky's parents had always taught her to respect elders. And she had to respect Doña Carmen Maria because, if not, Becky feared the old woman would walk down the street and report her incivility. Becky could see herself grounded until she was as old as Doña Carmen Maria herself.

"Let's play," Doña Carmen Maria suggested, the corner of her mouth lifting impishly.

Play! Becky thought. She could feel her own mouth sag and a groan rise from the back of her throat.

"You know how to play?" Becky asked.

"Like Tiger." The old woman giggled with a hand over her smile.

Becky was scared to say no. So she asked Doña Carmen Maria a second time—the old woman's answer was "Let's go, girl."

Becky thought, *Man, she sounds like Dulce, except she's way old.*

"Okay," Becky said. "You go first." She dropped the ball into the dust, and moved to give Doña Carmen Maria room to swing.

"Like Tiger," the old woman muttered. "I'm going to play like Tiger." She undid the top button of her sweater and pulled up her sleeves. She eyed the golf ball and the hole and told Queenie to be quiet. She struck the golf ball, which rolled smoothly and came within inches of going in. *"¡Casi!"* she yelled. She danced a jig that raised dust at her feet and approached the golf ball for an easy tap in.

Becky was impressed. But she figured it was beginner's luck. She dropped her own golf ball in the dust, positioned herself, wiggled her hips like she was dancing salsa, and swung her club. The golf ball raced like a rabbit past the hole.

"¡Qué lástima, muchacha!" Doña Carmen Maria snapped her fingers.

It took two more strokes before she got the golf ball into the hole. To her amazement, Becky found herself behind—three to two.

On the second hole, Doña Carmen Maria again struck the golf ball within inches of the hole. She smiled and shuddered. "When I warm up better, I'll get it in the first time."

Warm up? Becky wondered. The sun was cooking the back of her neck. Her tongue was thick from thirst.

On the second hole, Becky's putt sent the golf ball left and four feet from the hole. It took her three more strokes before the ball rolled in. She was down seven strokes to Doña Carmen Maria's four.

"I like this game," the old woman said when she made a hole in one at the third hole. "I'm going to be on TV with Tiger. You see, *mi'ja.*" She laughed and picked up Queenie for a quick smooch.

Becky struggled. Sweat poured from her face as Doña Carmen Maria pushed away to a commanding lead by the sixth hole. *How is this happening?* Becky wondered. *The old woman is at least a hundred years old! It isn't fair!* And it seemed ironic when at the seventh hole Doña Carmen Maria used her club like a croquet mallet. She laughed when the golf ball rolled into the hole.

"There are rules!" Becky snapped.

"*¿Cómo?*" Doña Carmen Maria asked.

Becky recalled her parents' warnings about respecting elders.

"Nothing," muttered Becky. She lined up her shot and in anger sent it skipping across the dusty ground and . . . into the hole!

"Way to go, girl!" Doña Carmen Maria said happily, her age-peppered hands coming together in patty-cakes. Then her mood darkened as she slowly sniffed the air. Her eyes became beady with worry. Queenie sniffed the air, too.

"*¡Ay, los frijoles!*" Doña Carmen Maria screamed. She let go of the golf club and scampered away with Queenie in the lead. But the old woman's foot got lodged in hole three, and she fell.

"*Ay!*" she chirped.

"Are you okay?" Becky asked.

Doña Carmen Maria didn't answer. She rose with a powdering of dust on her eyelashes and limped toward her house, yelling, *"¡Fuego! ¡Fuego!"* The old woman stopped and began to pat her sweater, as if she were on fire. *"¡Ay, mis llaves!"* She bent down and checked the pockets of Queenie's sweater. She cried that her parakeet, Banana, was going to be burned.

Becky boosted herself up onto the fence. There was smoke rising from the roof. "Ah, man," she whimpered. Doña Carmen Maria's house was on fire! "Fire!" Becky yelled, and she jumped over the fence, her golf club still in hand.

Doña Carmen Maria ran up the driveway, her arms flailing. She cried, "Banana! Banana!" She went to the backyard and rattled the back door.

"She's locked out," Becky said, and suddenly rued the day when her uncle had given her a set of golf clubs. Her parents would certainly blame her for keeping the old woman away from her house. They would scold that it was her fault Doña Carmen Maria's house was burned to the ground.

"¡Está locked!" Doña Carmen Maria cried. *"No tengo mis llaves. ¡Ay, Dios mío! ¡Están en la casa! En la* cookie jar. *¡No, no, en la mesa!"*

Becky pulled on the doorknob and yanked with all her might. The situation became worse when Queenie scooted through the doggie door.

"¡Ven!" cried Doña Carmen Maria. "Queenie! *Véngase.*" Her eyes were full of tears for her dog, her parakeet, and her house.

Becky yelled, "Step back!"

Doña Carmen Maria stepped back off the small landing.

"More!" Becky commanded.

Doña Carmen Maria stepped away and bumped into lawn furniture.

Becky brought the golf club high over her head and, eyes closed and shoulders hunched, let it fall hard. The window of the back door exploded and showered glass. The opening released a billowy dark cloud of smoke.

Becky coughed and, carefully, as she didn't want to cut herself on glass, pushed her hand through to fiddle the lock open. She covered her face as she stepped into the pantry area. She called, "Queenie! Queenie, come here." She could see the dog seated in the corner with a plastic hot dog between her paws. The dog's tongue was out and she was panting.

"Come here!" Becky yelled. She advanced three steps, her eyes tearing and her nose beginning to run. She didn't see any flames, just ash-colored smoke. But she could see the flames of the stove's burner—the pot of beans was burning away.

Queenie then rose, scratched herself, and disappeared from the kitchen into the living room.

Becky turned and went outside.

"¿Y Queenie?" Doña Carmen Maria asked.

"She won't come to me!" Becky cried. She lifted her face to the sky as she made out the sounds of a fire engine and then—was that Dulce's father's pickup truck?—the rattle of a vehicle's fender. The rattle seemed to grow louder and meaner. Becky pictured Dulce in the back of the pickup eating a red whip. She pictured Dulce with a fireman's helmet.

"Queenie!" Doña Carmen Maria called in a muffled voice. "¡Véngase!" She had stripped off a sweater and was holding it against her nose and mouth, like a bandit. She climbed the steps and disappeared into the smoke-filled kitchen before Becky could warn her not to go in.

"Ah, man," Becky wept. "¡Señora! Come out! You're going to suffocate!" Becky could hear Doña Carmen Maria bumping against a chair and then the twist of the knob on the stove—the burner was off. She then made out the hissing sound as Doña Carmen Maria put the ruined pot under the kitchen faucet. Her steps then ran across the linoleum floor and softened when she went into the carpeted living room.

Dulce's father's old pickup truck ground quickly up the driveway. Before he completely stopped, kids were leaping from the back of the pickup. Dulce was among them. She had a red whip licorice hanging from her mouth.

The kids ran toward Becky. One called, "Is anyone dead?"

Becky jumped at the thought. She pictured Doña Carmen Maria and Queenie all toasted in their sweaters. Their hair and fur were fried. Smoke was rolling off their bodies.

But Becky knew that wasn't their fate. The smoke had begun to clear, and she could hear Doña Carmen Maria cooing words of love to Queenie. Queenie produced two barks, and her dog tags chimed like bells.

Dulce's father hurried up the drive to the backyard. He told the kids to stay back and be careful with the broken glass. He entered the house, a hand covering his mouth, and opened the window over the kitchen sink. There were sounds of other windows opening and then the sounds of a fire engine rounding the corner.

"I'm in trouble," Becky bawled to herself. Tears filled her eyes, and she knew they couldn't put out her parents' anger when Doña Carmen Maria would later tell her story of golf and the burned pot of beans. Becky picked up her golf club, which prompted Dulce to say, "Let's play golf. I'll putt left-handed this time."

Becky propped her arms against her chest.

"Come on, girl!" Dulce reminded her that she had to practice if she wanted to be good.

"I hate golf!" Becky heard herself say.

"Don't say that," Dulce said. "It's funner than swimming." She told Becky how she had swallowed a lot of nasty water when she beat the boy staying underwater so long. She described how the water came out of her nose, plus *mocos*.

"That's stupid," Becky barked.

"Stupid?" Dulce said. She plunged a hand into her pants pocket and pulled out a soggy dollar bill. "He had to pay up when I won!"

Becky turned her back on Dulce and began to cry. She found herself running down the driveway. Her mother would be mad, and her father, and everyone in the world. She pictured her mother sniffing the air, thinking to herself, *Who burned the beans?*

Me! she answered in her mind. "Me! Me!" She pitched her golf club over the fence, and as she ran past the golf course, she felt her pockets for a golf ball. She flung it with all her might. The ball bounced and skipped and rolled into the sixth hole—a miracle shot at a time when it was just too late.

The Cadet

One early morning Richard Ortega stepped over a puddle formed by the one working sprinkler on the only green patch of his school's lawn. He shook a few dots of water from his shoe and examined the shoe's glossy tip: The last thing he wanted was a flaw in his dress uniform. It was the second Friday of the month, when a real army sergeant (retired) would evaluate their Junior ROTC battalion of middle school cadets.

"Dang," Richard muttered. Although the tip of the shoe might appear mirror-bright to some, Richard thought it was slightly dulled by those dots, which he raked off with his thumb. He considered rubbing his shoe on his pants leg and giving it a good polish. But he feared he would wrinkle the ironed crease of his pants, and he would then have two demotions to his self-respect. Instead, he cut across the campus to the boys' room, so he could give the shoe a good polish with a paper towel. But when he ventured into the restroom, which was dark from some missing overhead lights, he found the towel dispenser empty.

"Aw, man," he moaned. Richard then looked to the stalls, where he snagged a fistful of toilet paper. In a clipped step worthy of his rank as corporal, he advanced toward a sink, only to find two boys hovering around the glow of a cigarette.

"What?" one of the boys snarled. Smoke rolled from his nose like a dragon.

"You look like a janitor," the other boy said. Laughing, he revealed a wreck of badly stained teeth.

True, Richard's uniform was khaki colored, but he would argue that he looked nothing like a janitor. After all, the corporal stripes were attached to his epaulets and his left sleeve displayed the insignia of Battalion 238, a roaring lion. And what about the row of ribbons for conduct, parade, and academic excellence? Those two boys, denizens of dark corners, would never know the last. They would never even know the inside of a high school if they didn't shape up. That was Richard's assessment of those two losers, although he knew better than to mess with them. One was named Tyrone and the other Jared, both troublemakers with the grime of their dirty deeds embedded underneath their fingernails. When they spit, they left green splotches the size and consistency of pigeon droppings. Only last week the principal had collared them for scribbling graffiti on walls.

Richard backed away from the sink, not with the sharp military turn of a cadet but with the wariness of a boy watching out for his survival. He left the restroom and, for a moment, was startled by the hazy morning light that made him blink as his pupils struggled to adjust. He nearly ran into Desiree Sanchez, also a cadet but with the rank of sergeant. Desiree was in every class with Richard—except, of course, PE. But if she had been, she would have been the superior athlete, as she was tall, fast, and competitive. Her legs and shoulders were rocks. Running track, she would have left Richard in the dust. He was glad she was a girl.

"Hey! Watch where you're going—corporal!" Desiree scolded. "You almost stepped on my shoes."

"Oh, sorry, Desiree," Richard said. He glanced down at her polished shoes.

Desiree propped her hands on her hips. "*Sergeant* Sanchez. Not Desiree. That's just for when you and me are at the playground."

A surprised Richard gazed openmouthed at Desiree. *She pulled rank on me!* She didn't crack a smile that would have softened her eyes. In fact, her eyes darkened. Richard could not help but survey the two rows of ribbons and the red cord looped around one shoulder. He could only envy the dangling medal for marksmanship. His eyes were weak, but hers, he figured, were eagle sharp. After all, she was on the shooting team, while he was relegated to watching from the back wall of the downstairs armory.

"What are you looking at?" Desiree asked.

"Nothing." Richard knew she must be thinking that he was staring at her breasts. That wasn't the case, but he figured that he might insult her if he said he was admiring her ribbons and not her figure. Girls, he had concluded a long time ago, were weird. He didn't know what to say. "I was just—"

Desiree didn't allow him to finish. She turned away when she heard her name called.

He completed his thought in his mind: *I was just looking at your ribbons, Desiree—really.* He admitted to himself that he was envious of her rank and the display of hardware that went with it. He was also—he swallowed an unexplainable hurt—envious because she was a better athlete, and her family was nicer than his. Sure, she appeared hard, but her mother was sweet, not like—he swallowed again—his own mother.

His mother was moody. When she talked she never made eye contact. She was distant. She would ask the kitchen knife, "How was school?" She would ask the washing machine, "Did you return the videos on time?" She would ask the steering wheel, "Did you clean up your room?" His mother, he realized, suffered from something, and that something might be her husband, Richard's father, who had left them four years ago. His departure had been embarrassing for all of them. With the car unable to start, his father had ridden away on Richard's bike. His mother had called him a deadbeat, a no-good so-and-so, a shiftless rat. Richard was not proud to admit it, but he wished he had his bike, not his father, back.

Richard scanned the school campus, which was buzzing with students pouring out of two yellow buses that had just arrived. All of the students, it seemed to him, were dressed in loose sweatshirts and baggy pants, including the girls, whose lips were painted not rosy colors but earthy browns. He recognized a few other cadets. He suddenly felt a part of something meaningful. The first bell rang, and the cadets hurried up in a march, while the others—those in hooded sweatshirts and loose pants that revealed underwear—appeared to slow down. Richard even noticed that a few had turned around and started to leave the campus, absently dropping empty potato-chip bags and other debris. They had given up on school for the day. They had given up for good, for all Richard knew or cared. He wished they would go away, just like his father, and never be heard from again. The world would be a better place.

Richard went to English and then history. He had done his homework and volunteered answers to questions the teachers asked. His hand shot up like a spear, perhaps too eagerly because he heard someone snarl, "Teacher's pet cadet." He ignored the taunt. But by the time Richard was in social studies, he realized the activity of raising his hand had taken the ironed stiffness out of his sleeve. It was now pleated with wrinkles.

Finally, right before lunch, he had cadets, his favorite class. He was careful not to leave social studies in a hurry. He feared that someone might step on his shoes or that he might bump against others in the hallway, thus wrinkling his uniform. No, he intended to remain sharp for presentation. Only three weeks ago he had been promoted to squad leader, and he had an image to protect. He walked with his hands curled, as he anticipated falling into place with his squad.

Instead, Richard winced. He could see in his mind Rafael Ortega, the squad clown, chewing gum or maybe belching seconds after Cadet Major Kamakura would call "Attennnnnnnnnntion!" What was worse was that he and Rafael shared the same last name. It was too embarrassing for him.

The three platoons formed like molecules into squads. The cadets' stance was at ease until Cadet Major Kamakura, eyes slicing left, then right, sucked in gobs of air and called out, "Attennnnnnnntion!" Indeed, there was a skirmish in the four squads that made up Platoon C. Rafael, true to form, had not only burped but had taken his nastiness to a new level: He farted.

The entire C platoon laughed. In his squad someone said, "Pheew" and another bawled, *"¡Qué cochino!"*
Richard, however, stared straight ahead, his ears tuned
for a command. "Grow up," he remarked to himself.
He considered doing an about-face and pulling Rafael
from the squad, but Mr. Mitchell, the teacher, did that
for him. He tugged on Rafael's arm, and Rafael, still
jerking with laughter, was sent to the principal's office,
but not before he burped loudly and perfumed the air
with another blast.

Again the entire platoon—except Desiree Sanchez
and himself, the cadets with a future—began to sway
with laughter. But the laughter stopped when Mr.
Mitchell, eyes stoked with an angry fire, turned and
shouted, "Shuddup!" The four squads stiffened, though
a few cadets still bore remnants of smiles. But quickly
the cadets checked themselves completely, and not because of Mr. Mitchell's threatening voice but rather in
response to the approach of two true army soldiers.
The entire platoon had caught sight of them—and just
in time.

Wow, Richard thought. It was not only Sergeant
Moore but a real officer who had so much hardware
on his chest that Richard wondered how he could walk
straight up instead of bent over. The sergeant and the
officer shook hands with Mr. Mitchell, who left in the
direction of the principal's office—he was not through
with Rafael Ortega.

Cadet Major Kamakura, all seriousness, saluted first the sergeant and then the officer. The major made a command that Richard couldn't pick up, and Cadet Major Kamakura yelled, "Sirrrrrr!" and saluted. He then turned left, and called out, "Attennnnntion." He paused dramatically before barking, "Today, along with Sergeant Moore, we have the honor of welcoming retired Major Charles Wilson of Battalion Forty-three to inspect platoons."

Major Kamakura cut his eyes left, then right. "Does he have our respect?" he barked.

"YES, SIR!" the battalion yelled.

"Do we have the appropriate respect for Sergeant Moore?"

"YES, SIR!"

It was announced that the inspecting officer would also award a few ribbons. Richard couldn't think of any that he deserved but still imagined the major pinning one on his shirt. He imagined that the major, a veteran of many conflicts, would give off the scent of gunpowder or maybe a hand grenade.

Richard stiffened as the color guard walked in front of them, flags waving in the slight breeze. He felt pride, an emotion he tried to conjure up daily, though his school was not an easy place to do it. The lawn was small and ragged, the buildings old with leaky roofs, and the gymnasium condemned because it had been constructed decades before of brick, an earthquake hazard. These days the students had to play basketball on bent hoops with no nets.

After the presentation of colors, Cadet Major Kamakura ordered loudly, "Left face!"

The four platoons turned with precision. Again, Richard felt pride. The cadets, even the dumpy ones, would finally prove themselves in front of a real officer. Their cadet major called out, "Forward . . . MARCH!"

Cadet Captain Clayton, who was directly under Cadet Major Kamakura, chanted, "Your left, your left, your left, right, left."

They paraded for fifteen minutes while Major Wilson and Sergeant Moore huddled together and talked, indifferent, it seemed to Richard, to the three platoons' complicated maneuvers. But he realized it was not his place to assume what they were talking about. Maybe they were talking about the Raiders' loss to Tampa Bay on *Monday Night Football*. Maybe they were discussing the off-season trade of a baseball player. Maybe they were discussing those who didn't laugh at Rafael Ortega. That would be Desiree Sanchez and himself.

A few minutes later Richard discovered they were not talking about him at all. But he had gotten half of it right. They had been talking about Desiree Sanchez, who was awarded a medal for her marksmanship and was promoted to staff sergeant. *She's pulling away from me,* he thought. *I've been a corporal for more than five months. When will it be my turn?*

As Richard stood right behind Desiree, he could hear every piece of praise they offered her. He heard Major Wilson applaud her skills, her demeanor, her dedication. He saw him shake hands with Desiree before he saluted her. She saluted in return with a sharp snap of a starched sleeve. He felt envious. She was leaving him even further behind. *I'm never going to catch up,* he whined in his mind.

From the corner of his eye, he made out a land-locked sea gull watching Desiree's promotion before it turned its attention to an empty potato-chip bag. The bird fit its huge head inside the bag and was eating the flakes of someone else's cheap meal.

After school Richard left with three other cadets and passed Tyrone and Jared, who were leaning against the chain-link fence, smoking.

"Here come the janitors," Jared snarled. He flicked a burnt match at them.

Tyrone laughed. Smoke flowed from his mouth in one huge, dirty cloud.

The cadets ignored them, and within a block the three cadets—all corporals and squad leaders—were walking in step. Richard wanted to bring up Desiree Sanchez's promotion. But he gnawed his lip and swallowed the words that would have been something like the cheap argument "It's because she's a girl—that's why she got promoted!"

The three cadets walked in silence and then peeled away. Even alone, Richard marched with cadet-sharp steps as he turned up his street. Two kids on trikes stopped and watched him. He felt a glow of pride that showed in a smile. He nearly volunteered, "I'm a corporal," but he knew they wouldn't understand. Instead, he said, "Don't ride in the street."

Richard paused in front of his house. Through the front window, he could see his mother coiling up the cord of the vacuum cleaner. He could tell she was in one of her moods—her face was dark, her eyes deep and full of sorrow. A loopy curl fell in front of her face. Her movements and body language all said: *I'm sad.*

"Hey, Mom," Richard said lightly when he entered the front door, wiping his shoes loudly. He felt he had to assure his mother that he wasn't about to dirty the house with whatever stuck to the soles. He felt he had to turn her mood into something cheerful.

"Hi, Richard," she said to the vacuum cleaner she was lifting.

"I'll put it away, Mom." He hurriedly took the vacuum cleaner from her. He sniffed the air. "What are you cooking, Mom?" He forced up a smile.

"Soup," she answered. "Someone called today and hung up."

Richard swiveled his attention to the telephone in the living room.

"It was probably nobody," Richard argued.

"How come it rang, then?"

Richard offered no answer. He thought he should do his simple task and leave her alone until dinner. He headed down the hallway toward the closet. He placed the vacuum cleaner in the back, where his father's shoes still sat, dark and worn and nothing like his own shoes. He paused there for a moment. His mood seemed to grow sad. He listened to the sound of the refrigerator opening and closing, then the hard thud of what could be frozen hamburger on the kitchen counter. They were going to have hamburgers with their soup.

Richard was familiar with the closet. Once, when he and his cousin played hide-and-go-seek, while he was standing there in the dark, he discovered his father's army uniform. He was surprised because his father had never mentioned that he had served in the armed forces. His father had been a corporal, or so Richard gauged from the two stripes that ran along both sleeves. Two ribbons over the left breast pocket were evidence his father had also done something good. The ribbons were frayed from years of moth attacks. How he had earned them, Richard would never know. All because Father had ridden off on his bicycle.

Richard returned to the kitchen. He was right after all. They were going to have hamburgers in addition to soup. A big frozen block of ground round was on the counter. In an hour the meat would begin to defrost and shed its gray tears.

Richard double bagged canned goods—soups, pinto beans, SPAM, and fruit cocktail mostly—and handed them to a mother whose coat was too large for her. It was Saturday morning, and he was volunteering at a Presbyterian church. That kind of service was required if he wanted to earn a community service ribbon.

"Thank you," the woman said. Her smile was jagged.

Richard smiled. He tried to build up some light in his eyes. He tried to be kind and concerned, though those emotions were not with him right at that moment. Especially not after he noticed that her overly bright lipstick overran her mouth. She had the features of an unhappy clown.

Earlier in the morning, when his breath still hung in the cold air, he had been assigned to lug groceries from a truck into the church. He followed orders from a woman pastor who, like his mother, hardly looked at him when she spoke. Her inattention, however, gave him a chance to look at her: He noticed that the roots of her dyed hair showed white. And a portion of her left pinkie was gone.

"You can put the boxes there," she would say to the floor. "Could you get the broom?" she would ask the window, where a pair of pigeons peered in.

Richard was behind a wobbly table, bagging groceries and handing them over to families in need. To him most of the families suffered in other ways. Their noses ran, their clothes were dirty, and their jowls had the hound-dog look of sorrow. He caught himself swallowing sobs for them. He prayed that he would get a good job when he grew up and that he wouldn't have to descend the stairs of a church basement and open his arms for free food.

But that mood changed when he saw Rafael Ortega, the troublemaker cadet, come down the steps to the basement. He was leading his mother and three other children.

"Aw, man," Richard muttered as he gripped a dented can of pork and beans.

Rafael stopped, too. He looked back nervously at his mother and said something to her. She responded in Spanish, a language Richard should have known (everyone reminded him) but didn't. But he could tell that Rafael's mother was mad at him. Her Spanish was rapid-fire, her eyes smoldering. And what was that? A flat hand ready to rise up in a punishing slap?

Rafael turned and faced Richard.

"He's embarrassed," Richard whispered, and observed that Rafael was wearing his cadet pants. To Richard it didn't seem right for him to wear a part of his uniform on a Saturday. Then Richard had a revelation: *Maybe he doesn't have any other pants except his ca-*

det pants. That's why he's embarrassed. But, no, Richard thought. *His embarrassment has to do with his family having to ask for food.* Still, he was confused because Rafael's mother was fat. It appeared she ate a lot.

The family approached the table in one slow-moving herd. Richard snapped open a bag and was all ready to fill it with goods. He told himself, "Don't look up. Just fill the bag and get it over with." His hands worked quickly as he added soups, bags of pinto beans, boxes of Jell-O, cans of tuna, and instant coffee.

He handed the first bag to Rafael, who took it but refused to gaze up and meet Richard's eyes. Rafael turned away without a word, and his mother said something in Spanish, something not nice, because her words had the two other children stepping away from her apparent anger. They didn't want to get in the way if she started hitting Rafael. The mother then turned back and faced Richard, who was plying a new bag with goods. He didn't dare raise his eyes.

"*Gracias,*" the woman said without a smile and not much movement of her mouth. She waddled away. Her children, including Rafael, were standing by the entrance that would take them from the basement and back up the stairs.

Richard was glad when they left. He worked until two in the afternoon, bagging groceries and applying to his face a smile that he—and maybe others—could tell was not always sincere. He felt bad about that, his insincerity, and tried to make up for it by helping a grandmotherly woman with her groceries. She needed someone to lug them home for her. Home, she said, was only three blocks away.

"Watch your step," Richard warned as they climbed the steps of the basement. He couldn't hold her arm to help because he was carrying two heavy bags of groceries.

To Richard the world seemed full of too much light. He had to squint his eyes shut until the pupils adjusted. When he opened them, he was surprised to find the woman fitting a cigarette in her mouth. She lit it and took three quick puffs, followed by a long pull that collapsed her cheeks. When she released the smoke, it took the shape of a noose. She next licked her thumb and put the cigarette out with its wetness. The woman carefully cupped the cigarette into her hand and placed it back into her coat pocket.

"Which way?" Richard asked.

"That way," the woman answered, pointing vaguely. A cloud of smoke broke from her mouth.

The two walked in silence for three blocks. Richard tried to think of something to ask her, but his mind was disturbed by her smoking. *Where does she find money to buy cigarettes, anyhow?* he wondered. *Isn't she supposed to be poor and unable to afford such a trashy luxury?*

Finally he managed to ask a question he believed

might get them talking: "Have you always lived around here?"

"What?" the woman asked, cupping her wrinkled ear toward him.

"Are you from around here?" he tried. He was upset at the sight of an old ear that had heard truths and lies and—somewhere, at some time, by someone— words of love?

"Yeah, I live nearby." She pointed in the direction of a tall apartment building with torn awnings. Two men in greasy jackets were changing a flat tire.

"In that building?" Richard asked. He jerked his chin toward the apartment building.

"Yeah, I live nearby."

Richard pleated his brow with lines of confusion. He had to wonder if she was all right in her head. After that Richard just kept a slow pace, but in one weak moment he nearly asked that she hurry up. The bags of groceries were hurting his arms. Once he had to stop and place the bags on the hood of a car and rest. It was during this two-minute break that she took out her unfinished cigarette, lit it, and took a few puffs that had her mouth gathering into deep and dark lines. She then again wet her thumb and stubbed the cigarette against its moisture. It sizzled.

Richard was glad that he finally got to her place, which was not an apartment but a house. The front yard was full of weeds, and the grass was dead where a parked car had leaked oil. He climbed the steps ahead of her, placed the bags of groceries in front of the door, and waited for her to climb the steps.

"Let me help," Richard, a good cadet, said. He clomped down the steps and hooked his arm under hers, creating an image of a mother and good son to a passerby. At that moment he felt a sharp weight in her pockets—it took no smarts for Richard to figure that she had helped herself to a few cans without asking. Still, he wasn't about to say anything. He just wanted to get away. He waited for her to open the front door so he could say, "You're home! I gotta go."

"You can put the bags on the table," she told him. She shoved the door open and entered.

He bent down and picked up the two bags. Following close on her heels, he was overwhelmed by the stench of cigarettes and—he sniffed, nose moving like a rabbit's—an odor he recognized. Then he saw where it came from: What he imagined was a furry couch was actually layers and layers of cats. Their glowing eyes seized his attention. Three stood up, stretched with gaping mouths, and climbed down from the couch.

"Oh, man," Richard muttered.

"What?" the woman asked as she took off her hat. Richard could see the white roots of her dyed hair.

"Nothing," he said. He hurriedly set the grocery

bags on what he believed was the kitchen table. On the table lay two more cats, asleep, though their tails were twitching. His steps didn't disturb the sleeping cats. And the cats didn't spring awake when cans of soup dropped from the old woman's coat pocket with a loud bang—she had taken off the coat and hastily swung it onto a chair.

Richard picked up one of the cans that had rolled near his feet. A can of creamed corn. He set it on the table.

"I'm hungry," the old woman said. "I like vegetable soup."

Richard bit his lip. He didn't like her, and he didn't like the house. Three cats were rubbing against his ankle. "I have to go."

"Help me." Her eyes had a pleading look of someone clinging to a cliff.

Richard wondered what she meant.

"Change a lightbulb for me." She waved a hand toward the darkened hallway.

"Yeah, I guess," Richard answered lamely. He had to wonder if the lightbulb was in her head—she seemed dim.

Then a sound of water running in the bathroom made them turn their heads. They both held their breath.

"Is anyone home?" Richard asked. He was ready

to pitch a can of creamed corn if an intruder showed himself.

"What?"

Richard repeated himself. He asked if anyone was there.

"I didn't hear anything." The woman cupped her ear in order for its ancient hole to pick up a sound as quiet as a knock.

"I think there's someone in the bathroom," Richard said.

She winced. "Maybe . . ."

The bathroom door swung open. A voice called roughly, "Grandma?"

Instead of relaxing from hearing what only could be a familiar voice, her face grew tense. The old woman grew scared. She turned to Richard and, in a near whisper, repeated, "Help me." Scared, Richard backed away when her hand rested on his shoulder.

From the darkened hallway appeared Jared, the kid from school. Smoke was rolling from his nostrils. Jared stopped. He looked at his grandmother, then Richard, a fanglike snarl creeping from the corner of his mouth. He stepped into the dining room and, eyes still on Richard, asked his grandmother, "What's he doing here?"

Richard explained.

"He's a nice boy," the old woman added.

Richard stood nearly at attention, his hands curled at his sides, his shoes angled and pointed outward.

"Your grandmother asked me to help her," Richard said.

"Yeah, but you're done now, ain't you?" Jared walked around the table, and for a second, Richard thought Jared was going to hit him. But Jared just plunged his hand into his grandmother's pocket and brought out a crushed pack of cigarettes.

"Don't—" his grandmother started to say, but her hand instinctively came up and swatted those words from her lips.

Richard turned away, head down. *Let them fight over cigarettes. Let them put in their own lightbulbs.* Two cats, like sentries, stood by the door. Both of them were washing their paws with the buds of pinkish tongues.

He left the house. The sunlight had him squinting his eyes. This time, however, he wasn't hugging bags of groceries, and he was able to raise a hand to shield his sight. He appeared to be giving a cadet salute, and he realized that. He realized also that the world needed discipline and that maybe it was a soldier's duty to provide it.

"Why is it like this?" he asked himself. "Why are people like this?" His mind flashed on his father, who had disappeared on a bicycle, and then his mother, who was probably at the sink peeling carrots or potatoes. His mind flashed on Desiree Sanchez. He would never catch up with her.

"That's the way it is," he found himself saying.

He climbed down the steps and took a sharp left. Soon he was marching in a clipped step and wondering about that community service ribbon he would earn, imagining a future that did not include smoke billowing from bitter mouths.

The Sounds of Love

When Norma Lucero opened up her locker, she wasn't sorry to find that her flute was gone. In fact, she smiled and stomped her shoes, an action that made her skirt jump around her knees. And was that a rush of blood into her heart? She touched her heart, then her cheeks. Her temperature had risen.

"Yes," she said to herself. She raised a fist and repeated, "Yes." She closed the locker, turned, and leaned against it. Her smile was like a bright orchid on a cold winter day.

It wasn't that Norma hated playing the flute or the long hours of band practice in the musty basement of Franklin D. Roosevelt Middle School, a dingy room where the furnaces clanged, rattled, and messed up everyone's musical timing. And it wasn't that she hated looking like a nerd as she carried her instrument in a black case. No, the disappearance of her flute meant love: Samuel Ortega, a boy she liked a lot, had pulled her case from her grip the week before, and she'd had to run after him until he relented and gave it back. Now, she assumed, he had stolen it. Love was a kind of thief, she believed. Love involved taking something and giving it back.

She didn't have to dig deep into her memory to recall the day when Samuel had spit a mouthful of sunflower-seed shells and then asked, "Why don't you kiss me instead of that flute?" That a sunflower-seed shell stuck to his lower lip didn't destroy the beauty of that moment for her. It would soon fall off, and he would return to being the perfect boy for her. Sure, he was a little heavy, but wasn't she, too? Didn't that make them a perfect match?

That Samuel knew nothing about her music didn't keep her from liking him, either. "You'd like that, huh?" she told him, not too loudly, then giggled with a hand in front of her mouth. She had to admit that the way she pursed her lips when she played the flute was something like kissing—or so she believed. She had never kissed anyone, except Mom and Grandma, and her dad, when he was still around.

"Samuel's taken it," she told herself, and strode off to the cafeteria to buy some hot chocolate. "I'm sure of it."

"Hey," Rachael Duran called. Rachael, a member of band, was carrying a flute, too. "Let me copy your math."

Norma stopped in her pigeon-toed tracks. "Oh no," she moaned.

Rachael was a girl who wrote answers to quizzes up and down her arm, who pestered you with e-mail ("How do you spell Venice?" or "Who's Thomas Jefferson again?"), and who borrowed things and never gave them back. Norma noticed that Rachael was wearing Norma's barrette. She had lent it to Rachael during a parade march and never got it back.

"No, I can't," she yelled, and hurried toward the cafeteria to buy herself a morning treat. She let sixty-five cents, mostly in nickels, rain into the outstretched palm of the cashier. The cashier gave her a nickel back—she had paid too much.

When she blew on her hot chocolate, she saw in the reflection of that heavy brew that her lips were pursed—*Kiss, kiss, kiss*, she thought. Her giggling shook the surface of the hot chocolate into ripples. As she put her drink down on the table, she heard the sound of approaching footsteps. She put up her hand, as if stopping traffic.

"No, I said," she said to Rachael. "I can't let you copy my homework."

Rachael pouted. "Come on!"

"It's not right!"

"I'm your friend."

Friend? Norma thought angrily. *A pest, you mean. A bug in my ear. A foxtail in my sock.*

"I won't ask except this one time. I promise." Rachael crossed her heart to make her point.

"I said no." Norma shouldered her backpack, picked up her hot chocolate, and walked away, indifferent to Rachael's snarl. "You better watch your back, girl."

Norma had been in such a good mood. Sip-sip-sipping from her hot chocolate. She had had the best thing she owned, her flute—*sip-sip*—taken from her by Samuel Ortega. What a guy! *Sip-sip.*

She fought her way through a crowd of students exiting through the glass doors of the cafeteria into the yard. She perched, knees together, on a cement bench, where she dreamily watched the steamy hot chocolate. When she exhaled, she saw her breath hang in the frosty air of midwinter.

"He likes me!" she exclaimed. She smiled. "Why else would he steal my flute?"

She had never had a boyfriend. She didn't even have many friends, and those friends were at church. In elementary school she had spent most of her time alone under a tree, where she read books. Her best friend then was Melissa Campbell, who, like Norma, was a little heavy. Their knees were pink, as were their faces and chubby little hands. Any kind of exertion made them pink—even climbing the three steps to their bungalow classroom. Together she and Melissa had spent a lot of time combing the manes of their My Little Ponies. They combed and combed them until the nylon hair fell out.

Norma's ears perked up when she suddenly heard a flute call above the sounds of shuffling students and skateboards. She stood up, the folds of her skirt falling out evenly. "Samuel?" She swallowed the rest of her hot chocolate in three quick gulps and grabbed her backpack, which was as heavy as an anchor—the math and biology books alone were as heavy as gym weights.

She walked in the direction of the sound.

"Samuel, give it back!" Of course, she was prepared to run after Samuel. She liked the idea of a chase on a cold morning.

"Samuel, you're going to be in big trouble!"

Norma made her way quickly through the students, some of whom were holding cups of hot chocolate. She thought she could still make out the sounds of her flute but wasn't sure. When the bell rang, the huddling students broke apart and headed noisily off to class.

"Samuel!" she called one last time. She imagined her voice as a flute, and imagined Samuel answering back. "Samuel, it's time for you to give it back!"

But Norma stopped when she saw Rachael seated at a bench and rushing answers to her math homework onto binder paper. She had gotten Jason Harvey to share his homework. Jason, Norma knew, wasn't good at math. He wasn't good at anything except basketball. Rachael finished copying Jason's homework and gave him a kiss. Her tongue, like a fat worm, touched Jason's tongue.

Norma's hand flew to her mouth to hold back a groan. *How disgusting*, she thought.

When band rehearsal was canceled, Norma stayed at school to do homework in the library. But first she wandered around the school grounds and hallways in search of Samuel. She checked the basketball court and metal shop. She had even hollered into one of the boys' bathrooms, "Samuel!" She was embarrassed when the janitor came out with a pipe wrench in his hand.

Norma had seen Samuel earlier in the day walking across the school grounds to deliver, she suspected, attendance slips. But she was seated in biology with a dissected frog in her hands and was in no position to scream out the window, "Hey, where's my flute?" And she had seen him at lunch surrounded by pimply boys stomping on their milk cartons. But she dared not confront him with his friends standing around.

In the library Norma did some of her homework and walked home at three-thirty, kicking through leaves that resembled soggy cereal. But she didn't go straight home. No, she stopped at Baskin-Robbins 31 Flavors—double chocolate, she discovered after trying all the flavors, was her favorite. She stopped at the ice-cream store to see if Samuel might be there with one of his friends. He wasn't, though her heart did jump when she heard the sound of a flute.

"Samuel," Norma whispered, then pulled her long hair in front of her face to hide her giggles. "It's the radio." She looked up at the ceiling and caught sight of a speaker with tiny, tiny holes. She placed a hand over her mouth and proclaimed, "I'm in love. I have to be!" She didn't care if the young man behind the counter heard her, or the woman who had just entered.

At home she found three messages on the message machine. Two were for her mother, and one was from Rachael, who wanted to know if she had sheet music for "Here Comes the Bride." She pressed the delete button in anger, as if she were squishing a mosquito.

"She's such a pest!" Her mood had soured.

She went into the kitchen, where she read a note from her mother: *Take the frozen chicken out of the freezer and put it in the sink. At 5:30 peel the carrots and potatoes, and dice the celery. Home at 6:00. Love, Mom.*

Soup. Chicken soup.

Norma had heard that chicken soup was good for your soul, and at that hour of the day, she was beginning to think that she might slurp up a big bowl and be cured of everything that ailed her. Only a half hour before, she had been feeling pretty, and then she realized that she might have to face her mother's anger if her flute had really been stolen, not just swiped by her lover boy, Samuel Ortega.

"But he has got to have it," she said, then jumped when the telephone rang. When she picked it up, it was Rachael.

"Hey, do you have—"

Norma cut her off. "No!"

"Gee, don't get so mad, girl." She hung up without a good-bye.

That night there was no soup to make her feel better. Instead, it was a chicken lathered in creamy sauce. Under the sauce, there were bits of mushrooms, a food that Norma despised. She rounded them up like they were enemies and scooted them around the edge of her plate. Later she would scrape them down the garbage disposal without mercy.

The next day she finally confronted Samuel at a drinking fountain. She decided to be nice. She used her mouth like a musical instrument and asked in a lilting voice, "Do you have my flute?" She asked this while her left hand held her right, and her body twisted, slightly.

"No," he answered bluntly.

Norma noticed that some of his breakfast—grease from eggs and bacon?—was splattered on the front of his shirt. His dark hair was uncombed. The knees of his pants were stained green with grass.

"You don't?" she asked meekly. Her left hand dropped the right hand. The courtship, it seemed, was off.

Samuel looked into her eyes and bit his lower lip. Finally he said, "Norma, quit following me."

Norma rocked on her heels.

"You do it every day."

"What do I do?"

"Pester me."

Hurt, she staggered backward. All last night she had lain in bed thinking of him. She dreamily conjured up his hair, the tenderness of his teddy bear eyes, and his voice that went up and down, not unlike a bird's, or that of her missing flute. All night she had pictured the two of them at Baskin-Robbins 31 Flavors sampling every delicate flavor. They were lapping the ice cream from the same cone, which, for her, was kind of like kissing. Their tongues almost touched, almost became flavored with something like love.

"I'm not following you!" Norma shot back.

Samuel grimaced. "Norma, I don't like you." He judged her response before he sucked in a lot of air. "I mean I like you like, you know . . ."

She did know. He liked her as a friend, or maybe just a classmate. She felt her heart shatter and spill gallons of blood. Yes, that was it! She was bleeding inside! She turned and walked away, her head down for a moment, then up again because she had to keep her pride.

"I don't care," she heard herself say, and she ventured into the cafeteria to get her morning hot chocolate. Tears blurred her vision, but she knew the route. Plus, the breakfasty smells of hot chocolate and doughnuts led the way.

"I hate him," she sniveled, and wiped the warm salty tears that had meandered down her cheeks. She sat alone at a table, where she composed herself and then, suddenly, punched her backpack three times. Feeling better, she got up and got herself some hot chocolate.

"He's a pig," she whispered. *Sip-sip.* "One day he'll see." *Sip-sip.* "I'm going places, and he's not!" *Sip-sip.*

When she saw Rachael coming into the cafeteria— Jason Harvey was at her side, his arm in hers—she hurried outside into the yard, fighting against the tide of students entering.

"I hate school," she moaned. She sat on the cement bench, alone. A pigeon visited her and stared her straight in the eye. It scratched and pecked at the ground. The pigeon soon left when it received no shower of bread crumbs or potato chips. But two sparrows arrived at her feet. Their chirps had the sound of flutes. They also sounded to her like rusty latches, but she preferred thinking of them as little flutes.

"What are you saying?" Norma asked.

Chirp, chirp.

"Are you, like, boyfriend and girlfriend?"

Chirp, chirp.

When the first bell rang, the birds flew into the bare wintry tree. Norma got up, spilled her hot chocolate on the cement, and started toward her first class. She imagined that the two sparrows were boyfriend and girlfriend. She imagined that they would dart down from their branch, drink, and maybe wash themselves in the sweetness of romance.

Mr. Burrows lifted off his eyeglasses and peered at Norma. He wanted to hear it again. He wanted to know where her flute was.

"A boy stole it," Norma answered. Her arms were across her chest. A curtain of bangs half hid her face.

"'A boy stole it,'" he said slowly as he slipped his eyeglasses back on. His eyes themselves grew large and luminous. "Did you hear that, class?" He got up and started to pace in front of the band members.

Some of the boys laughed. Only one girl laughed, and that was Rachael, whose arm was scribbled with answers to the next period's geography quiz. Her laughter revealed a wad of blue gum on the back of her molars. It also revealed that Rachael was truly not Norma's friend.

"It's not funny," Norma said without turning to Rachael, even though they sat next to each other on squeaky metal folding chairs.

Rachael raised her hand, her bracelet jangling like

a tambourine. The geography notes resembled tattoos and were revealed to the class.

Mr. Burrows's eyes got bigger behind his eyeglasses, his way of saying, *Yes?*

"I got an extra flute at home," Rachael said. She told the teacher that she could bring it tomorrow.

Yuck, Norma thought. *I have to put my lips to the mouthpiece of her flute?* She closed her eyes and pictured Rachael and Jason Harvey kissing. She pictured their tongues touching.

It was settled. Rachael would lend Norma her extra flute. It was also settled that the band members would meet, rain or shine, in front of city hall on Saturday for the Presidents' Day parade.

Rachael's hand went up.

Mr. Burrows lifted his shaggy eyebrows.

"What presidents are we marching for?" she asked.

Mr. Burrows sucked in his lower lip and then spat out, "All of them. But especially President Lincoln."

Out of habit Rachael wrote that piece of information on her palm. No telling when that answer might come in handy.

They would march with members of Hamilton Middle School. Like their own middle school, Hamilton had few members in the band. Their own band had three trumpets, two flutes, a trombone, a dented tuba, a glockenspiel that gave off the sounds of doorbells ringing all at once, a bass drum carried by a small boy, and three snare drums that always got all the attention from passersby. Together they still didn't have enough members to make up a true marching band. And neither school had uniforms. Hamilton Middle School sported sweatshirts—green and white ones, Norma recalled—or maybe blue and white. Her own school—Franklin D. Roosevelt—had red and white ones, with a picture of an ancient battleship.

Mr. Burrows spent time discussing the march. To do that, he called band members into the yard, where he first demonstrated a sort of cadet march, but with a swagger.

Three boys laughed. It struck them that their teacher looked like a girl as his legs kicked up in a march.

"Do you get it? We've done this before—remember?" Mr. Burrows was unaware that the boys were making fun of him.

The band members nodded. They were then pushed into four lines—the flutes and glockenspiel up front, and the trombone and trumpets in the second row. The tuba had its own line, and the snare drums and bass drum filled out the last line.

"Now march slow, and listen to each other's steps." He stood in front, walking backward and waving a baton. Occasionally he would look where he was going, but his attention was drawn mostly to the band members. "It's all coming back, no? Remember when we marched last year for Columbus Day?"

Norma felt stupid. She had no flute to bring to her mouth.

"Okay, that's not bad. Let's try 'Stars and Stripes Forever.'" Mr. Burrows ordered the band to attention and, after inspecting the lines, called out, "One, two, three, and—"

The band started playing, the beat of their instruments moving everywhere but in time. Their music was the sound of a car crash, or a pyramid of cans falling all at once. It was the sound of pipes falling off a tall rack, or a kettle whistling on a stove. It was the death moan of a Scottish bagpipe.

"Stop, stop, stop!" Mr. Burrows's chest heaved. He stared angrily at the trumpet players, then at the tuba. He let them know that they had better play better. "Let's start again." He waved his baton and called out, "Now one, two, three, and—"

This time the musicians fell into a reasonable tempo. Mr. Burrows smiled. It was imperfect for sure, but good enough.

But Norma was not smiling. She was marching with the band members but had nothing to contribute except a woeful look.

Still, as Mr. Burrows waved his baton, the band members became confident, and even proud, the boys parodying the swagger of Mr. Burrows that had had them laughing only a few minutes before. The roll of

the snare drums brought out a few lingering students
and teachers from the classrooms. They watched silently
as the band marched up the yard and then back down.

This is stupid, Norma thought. *Everyone's watching
me.* She believed that everyone—students and teachers, plus the afternoon janitors—was watching her, the
only one without an instrument. It got even worse.
Samuel Ortega, the boy who had spurned her, was
watching, too. He was holding a metal trash can by its
handle. He was picking up litter as a punishment for
something. Norma wanted to believe that it was for being mean to her. When Samuel started to bang the side
of the trash can, Mr. Burrows threw him the dagger of
a mean look. He stopped at once and continued to pick
up litter.

"Very good!" a beaming Mr. Burrows called out.
"Very, very good." He gave a command to march in
time, and then a forward, then flank left, then flank
right.

They marched until the afternoon became shrouded
in dusk. Norma had nothing to do but march and think
about love. Like everyone else, she wanted a boyfriend,
and wanted to go places with him—a movie, a park,
maybe to a lake where they could rent a boat. But she
had no boyfriend to hold, nor a flute, that chrome instrument that could send a beautiful melody up into
the air. Her fingers tapped at her sides, as if she were

playing a flute, as if she were suddenly involved in the music echoing throughout the school yard.

After band practice Norma went into the principal's office and cried into the comfort of her palms. She told Mrs. Conway that her flute was lost and almost whimpered, "Stolen."

"Let's look right now," Mrs. Conway suggested. Her eyes cut a glance at the clock. It was 4:30, late. She prodded Norma outside her office and into the hallway. Mrs. Conway's shoes rapped like gavels in the empty hallway.

"Where are we going?" Norma asked.

"The place where lost things go," Mrs. Conway answered mysteriously. She also told Norma that she should have reported the missing flute sooner.

Norma wanted to tell her she thought that Samuel Ortega had taken it from her locker, but her explanation would have been too complicated, if not false. Plus, she realized, he was already being punished for something.

Mrs. Conway tried three keys before she had success in turning the knob. When she pushed open the door, Norma faced a treasure of things that had been lost and never claimed—backpacks, lunch boxes, basketballs, coats and jackets, sweaters and sweatshirts, and—what was that?—a stuffed frog holding up a tiny umbrella? There were skateboards, shoes, skates, a box of eyeglasses, girlish umbrellas pink as flowers, and a flag of Great Britain. There were lots of books. There was also a trumpet and a black case, just like the kind she carried her flute in.

"Is this it?" Mrs. Conway asked.

Norma ran her hand over the case. "No." Tears filled her eyes and spilled down her face. She told Mrs. Conway about the Saturday march for Presidents' Day and how she had nothing to play.

"Then take it," Mrs. Conway said.

"But it's not mine."

"It's yours now." She wiped the tears from Norma's cheek.

Norma's hand reached up, and her fingers wrapped around the handle. When she pulled the case off the shelf, dust rose into the dark air. Mrs. Conway and Norma took turns sneezing as they walked down the hallway.

Norma left a message on Rachael's answering machine, informing her that she had a flute and not to bother bringing an extra one to the parade. She was so glad that she didn't have to put her lips on something touched by Rachael's lips. The thought made her shudder.

Norma cleaned the flute in her bedroom. It was old for sure, and pitted with rust marks and dented in places. But the keys worked nicely. She pressed the

mouthpiece to her lips and blew a long A. She worked
the keys as she played her exercise of "Do Re Mi." She
then started playing a sorrowful Japanese melody called
"Dawn in a Stone Garden," a melody that touched her
deeply. The day had been a long one. She would have
kept playing, but she heard a key in the front door—
for a second, she pictured the principal, Mrs. Conway.
But it was her mother, she knew. It was Friday night,
which meant pizza and maybe a video.

"Hi, Mom!" Norma called when her mother pushed
open the front door.

When Norma ran into the living room, ending with
a slide on the wooden floor, she discovered her mother
balancing pizza in her right hand.

"Hey, girl," her mother said. She tossed her car keys
onto the coffee table. "What are you doing?"

"Practicing for the parade." The old flute was in her
bedroom. She didn't want to risk upsetting her mother
by confessing that she had lost her flute.

Her mother asked if she was hungry.

Norma touched her stomach. That simple touch
produced a growl from the depths of her stomach.

"Let me make a quick salad," her mother said, and
rushed off to the kitchen.

No, it wasn't a video night but a night of girl talk.
After the salad was made and the pizza reheated in the
microwave, the two sat on the living room floor. The
house was quiet, and for a while the two, exhausted

from the day, were quiet. After her second slice, Norma asked, "Mom, will I ever have a boyfriend?" Norma amazed herself by her boldness. She and her mother had never talked about boys—or men for her mother, who sometimes sighed about her single status. Norma's question came up when her mother was bringing a forkful of salad to her mouth.

"Sure you will," her mother said after she cleared her throat. She set her fork down.

"But I'm, like, you know, chubby."

"No, you're not, honey. And anyway, everyone finds someone." Her mother looked off dreamily, as if she were looking for someone for herself.

"Were you and Dad boyfriend and girlfriend for a long time?" More bravery as Norma picked up a third slice. "Was it, like, love at first sight?"

"For a long time," her mother answered. "Two years. And yes, it was love when I first saw him." She explained that she first saw him when he was dancing with another girl. She didn't care. She knew that she was going to get him. But she would never believe that she would lose him years later to the same girl he had held in his arms—Betty Ugly Face, her mother called her.

"Did you have other boyfriends?"

Her mother smiled. "Lots." She let the word *lots* grow big in significance. Then she laughed with her hand over her mouth. Her mother confessed that was a fib.

Norma waited for her mother to finish laughing and then asked, "You sure? You sure I'll have a boyfriend?"

"Of course! You'll have lots." She then eyed the pizza. "But what you won't have is more pizza—the last slice is mine."

Norma went to bed early and stared up into a ceiling that was black, black, black. She thought for a while that it was like the night sky, but realized that the sky had stars and, beyond the stars, a heaven brilliantly lit with God's love. She rolled onto her side and went to sleep, with the feeling that love was possible. Hadn't her mother said so?

The next morning she dressed in her school sweatshirt, practiced on the old flute while standing over the floor furnace, and turned down a ride to city hall from her mother. She jumped over rain puddles and felt a happiness that made her light-headed. The sun broke through the February sky and lit the streets with a glare that nearly hurt her eyes.

She uncased her flute and played it on her way to the parade. People watched her and smiled. She lifted her head and trilled her flute at the birds. Her happiness wasn't even dispelled when she saw Rachael, who was licking her fingertips and rubbing something from her hand—an answer she no longer needed?

Mr. Burrows was talking with the band coach from Hamilton Middle School. They suddenly jerked with a laughter that made their bellies bounce over their belts. They patted each other's shoulders and turned to the mingling band members. They called them into squads.

"Come on, let's hurry," Mr. Burrows barked.

The two schools assembled into one band, with each Hamilton student standing next to a Roosevelt student. They took their position behind a platoon of soldiers in chrome helmets. In front of the platoon stood a somber color guard with the flags of California and the United States whipping in the wind.

"We're going to play what you know—'Stars and Stripes Forever' and 'This Land Is Your Land.'"

They practiced both tunes as Mr. Burrows winced dramatically. He covered his ears to make his point. "Let's do better, boys and girls. I know you're not used to each other, but you can do better." The Hamilton band members looked at the Roosevelt band members, and the Roosevelt band members returned their confused looks. They shrugged and smiled. It apparently sounded okay to them.

They practiced for ten minutes. They would have practiced longer, but the parade was about to begin. The parade marshal, a man dressed as President Lincoln, called on them to get ready.

Norma gazed behind her at a baton unit in red glittery outfits. The very young girls—the five- and six-year-olds—were up front, and the older, more glamorous girls in their midteens were in the back. Norma noticed that some were chewing gum.

She then noticed the boy next to her. She had first seen him when Mr. Burrows was yelling at them, and he was running a rag down the throat of his flute.

He smiled at her, shivering.

She thought he was cute and just like her—a little chubby.

"It's cold, huh?" he remarked. He hugged himself for emphasis. He chattered his teeth and said, "Brrrr."

Norma flushed. She thought he was so cute. Was this love at first sight? Like when her mom first saw her dad?

"Yeah, it's pretty cold," she agreed. She then called in return, "Brrrr." She had never used that sound, but then, she had never been standing next to a boy that might like her.

"What's your school like?" he asked. His teeth were white and straight, and his eyes clear and sincere.

"Big," Norma answered, throwing out her arms. She touched her hot cheek. *Yes, it's happening—it's love at first sight.* She began to wonder how far Hamilton Middle School was from her school. Was it a mile away? Across town?

"Norma!" Mr. Burrows called. "Let's pay attention, young lady."

She parted her bangs and, standing on tiptoe so

that she could see over the trombones, apologized, "Sorry, Mr. Burrows."

Her attention was drawn to Mr. Burrows and the drum major, a boy from Hamilton. He brought a shiny whistle to his mouth as he marched in place and in cadence with the platoon of soldiers in front of them. He blew once, then filled the air with a series of rhythmic blows that had the band marching. He twirled around, baton in hand, and inspected the band. Suddenly they were part of a parade in honor of presidents who at that moment didn't matter to Norma. She felt dizzy with happiness. What could it be but love?

Norma turned and smiled at the boy, who returned her smile before he brought his flute to his mouth.

"It's happening," she told herself. "I'm falling in love."

Because her flute didn't have a clip to hold sheet music, she followed his sheet music. She noticed that he played well, and marched well. And if he didn't play or march in cadence, who cared?

Norma trilled her flute on a high note, and, she noticed, the boy next to her returned her trill. *We're like birds,* she thought, *one lovebird talking to another.* She trilled her flute at him again, and again he responded with a trill. Her heart thumped. For years she had heard that romance had something to do with the heart, but she never believed it. Now she could see that it was true!

Norma felt pretty. She eyed the crowds lining the streets. The little kids were waving and some adults were clapping. When a boy began to wave frantically, as if he were drowning, she narrowed her eyes at the figure. Was it Samuel Ortega? It was! She made a face and, shrugging, explained to her new friend, "Just some pest from school."

The traffic up ahead slowed. The drum major turned and had them march in place. A wind lifted the leaves from the gutters and made them swirl and dance overhead. The sun disappeared behind clouds gray as elephants.

"Brrrr," the boy said to Norma.

"Brrrr," she said in return, though her cheeks were pink, a sign that she was anything but cold.

Teenage Chimps

Because I was broke and in the middle of a dull summer, I sat on the front porch playing heads-you-win, tails-you-lose with a bottle cap. I had drunk my last cream soda and followed it up with a banana that I unzipped with a fingernail. I tossed the peel into the flower bed. I sprinkled a few drops of soda on the porch and—*presto!*—ants appeared with their antennae waving like knives. I peered down at the chain of ants and wished I could reduce myself to their size and follow them to their hole. I wondered how they lived, those little ants, and felt great pity for them when I thought about how dearly they paid when a shoe smashed their guts.

But the ants were eventually boring. I flicked a bottle cap that went sailing onto the lawn, then tried to see if I could spit and hit the bottle cap. No luck. Spitting just made me thirsty. I got up, went inside the house for a drink of water, and returned in time to find this *mocoso* kid on a bicycle riding by. He yelled, "Hey, *Chango!*"

I jerked up my head in greeting.

The kid circled back and asked as he sped by, "How come you don't live in a zoo?"

At last an opportunity to shake off my boredom. I yelled that his parents, the hyenas, wouldn't let me. I stood up and yelled, "No, wait a minute! It's because your fat elephant mom won't make room for me."

The kid laughed as he gave me the finger and rode away doing a wheelie. His skinny shadow followed behind.

That little *mocoso* on the bike had it right. You see, I was once a boy, like any other, but I slowly turned into a chimpanzee when I was thirteen.

One morning I woke up craving bananas. When I jumped out of bed, I noticed that my arms hung a little closer to the ground. *Dang,* I thought, as I walked, arms dragging, to the bathroom. In the mirror I saw that my ears stuck out a little bit and my lower lip hung down. My nose was flat; my face, furry. Time to start shaving. I had the special gift of baring my teeth all the way to the gums. I had known ever since I was a little kid that I wasn't going to grow up to be a *GQ* model but a monkey.

My mother had always called me a monkey when I was really little because I used to bounce on the bed and couch, and climb the peach tree in the yard.

"Chango, stop that!" she would yell. "This is a house, not a zoo!"

Then again, Mom appreciated that I was cute as a chimp. She sold Avon products and would take me with her door-to-door through the rich part of town. When those doors opened, the homeowners, suspicious of peddlers, would scowl at my mother. Who wants anybody coming to your house selling stuff that don't work? Perfume only sweetens how you smell, not your personality. Then the owners' eyes would settle on me, a little monkey boy at my mother's side. Their faces would break into smiles, and in we went to the living room, where my mom would set bottles on the coffee table. That's how we got by in our family—Mom out selling Avon and sometimes sets of electric carving knives.

Meanwhile, Dad worked on cars in our driveway. He was a terrible mechanic who read Toyota manuals to repair Hondas, and Honda manuals to repair Volvos. The cars worked—or almost worked—when they pulled into our driveway. But by the time he finished with them, they would barely cough alive. The mufflers shot out blue smoke that brought tears to your eyes. Dad would scratch his head and leave oil in his already oily hair and mutter, *"¿Quién sabe?"*

But Dad ran away with a woman whose car he actually fixed—he replaced the starter and off they went in a Miata convertible that purred like a kitten. That was two years ago. Now I'm fifteen and more chimp than ever. I would be really lonely, except I have one friend who turned into a chimp when he was thirteen, too. His name is Joey Rios, a former wrestler in middle school. But he had to stop wrestling because every time he pinned an opponent, he would jump on the other guy's back and beat his own chest. He would let out a loud chimp scream that bounced off the gym's rafters. Coach said he was making too much noise pollution.

Joey and I hung out together in high school, sad that there were no monkey bars to keep us busy during break. There were no chimp girls, either. No one liked us. They would shove us out of the way, warning, "Don't slip on your bananas" or "How come your arms are so long?"

So Joey and me hung out behind a backstop, our eyes sometimes peering through the knotholes at the students having regular lives, you know, like girlfriends, clubs, after-school car washes, skateboarding, and playing in the band. We would hang out by the backstop looking at old *National Geographics*.

There was one teacher who felt sorry for us, but he got it wrong. Trying to be nice, he sometimes offered us bananas. It was sort of insulting. We would take the bananas, thank him, and walk away with them stuffed in our pockets like pistols. But most teachers just looked through us, even if we raised our hands to answer a question. Excited, I would mouth, "I know the answer. I know the answer." One day I realized how long my armpit hair was. From then on I kept my arms at my side.

My name is Ronaldo Gonzalez, better known as Ronnie. Joey and me are buddies for life. When we walk, we walk in step. When we look in the mirror, we see that we're the same, though Joey's ears stick out just a little bit more than mine. We're the only chimps we know who can do math, read a book, and speak both English and Spanish in a tree. But I wasn't in a tree when Joey rode up on his lowrider bicycle. I was on the porch.

"Joey!" I yelled, and jumped up and down in happiness.

Joey tossed his bike aside and beat his chest. He gave me a chimp smile. "I found some girls like us," he announced breathlessly.

"What do you mean?"

"Chimp girls. I saw them over by the canal."

I swallowed at the prospect of holding hands with a chimp girl. Chimp girls for us? Really? I pictured us walking hand in hand as our arms dragged on the ground. I pictured me letting my date take a bite out of an apple, and then me taking a bite out of the apple. After every fourth bite, I would get a kiss.

"You're lying, huh?" I asked. *Maybe he's trying to fool me*, I thought.

"Nah, chimp, I'm not." Joey expressed a hurt look. He scratched his armpit.

With me on the handlebars, we bicycled to the canal, where sometimes Joey and me swam, our toes never touching bottom because of the glass and junk that lay there. One time a car was submerged there, and I recognized it as one my dad had worked on. I figured the owner and a few of his buddies just rolled it into the canal and walked away.

At the canal we didn't find any chimp girls. We rode up and down the sandy banks and only found toads sitting on rocks. Lizards darting between the brush. Crickets making that cricket noise. A dead bird with a string of ants crawling from its eyes lay near a burger wrapper.

"They were here," Joey said. "Really." Sad, he produced an amazing pout.

I believed Joey. I kicked a three-inch hole in the sand and toed the dead bird into its little grave. I buried it by kicking sand in its face. I figured the sand wouldn't hurt him now. To me it was a disgrace that a poor dead bird should have no place to rest its twiggy bones.

We sat on the edge of the canal. We were more lonely than ever. We watched bluegills surface and mouth the dirty water. One fish seemed to throw up its food and then eat it again.

"I'd hate to be a fish," I said, disgusted.

"Yeah," Joey lamented. "But I hate being a chimp."
He asked me if I remembered being a regular kid.

A regular kid?

"Yeah," I remarked, and tossed a rock into the water. The fish moved heavily toward the descending
rock. I told him how I remembered being a baby in
my crib and how at night I used to stare out the window. Stars hung in the sky. I confessed to Joey how I
thought the stars were looking at me. Then, later, just
after I turned into a chimp, I told my mom about the
stars I used to see from my crib. Mom made a face
that wrinkled her mouth. She said the stars didn't care
about me or anyone else. She said that while splashing
Avon cologne on her throat and some on me because,
she said, my fur smelled wet.

"That's mean," Joey moaned.

"Yeah," I said, stirring my hand in the sand. I was
about to tell Joey about really neat clouds I had seen
from my window when some kids from school appeared on their dirt bikes. They had turned into rhinos. They were huge, and each sported a single horn
on its forehead.

"Whatta you chimps doing?" Cory snarled as he
tossed his bike aside. Cory used to be my friend in first
grade, but when I wouldn't join him and pee against
a wall, he beat me up. He said to keep away from him
until the end of time.

"Nothing," I said weakly.

Joey stared at the ground. I knew he was sizing up a place to fall if Cory and his friend—I forget his name—decided to push us around. Joey and I had learned that when a bully started to hit us, we could fall to the ground and pretend we were hurt. It seemed like we did that a lot. I don't know what Joey thought when he was on the ground, but I remembered the stars from my crib and wished someone really nice—like God—would come down on one of them and save us. But the only stars I saw were when I got smacked in the face. It hurt a little, but not too much. Now Cory stood in front of us. The horn on his forehead was shiny with pimples.

"I feel like beating you up," Cory said. His hands closed naturally into fists.

"You already did that," I said.

"When?"

"Last week," I lied.

Cory seemed to think about it. "Oh yeah, that's right." Then he walked over to the canal and unzipped his pants. He peed with his face turned skyward. His rhino friend did the same.

"What you chimps doing?" Cory's friend asked after he finished polluting the canal water.

"Waiting for girls," Joey answered honestly.

Neither Cory nor his friend laughed very long. Just a couple of grunts from their rhino mouths. I knew why. They were lonely, too, these huge rhinos who

desperately wanted to find two girls. I imagined them
clacking their horns together in friendship and love.

"Did you kiss them and stuff?" Cory asked. His eyes
were wet and wild, and he was hoping that something
exciting had happened.

"Not really," Joey said.

"What do you mean 'not really'? You did or you
didn't."

Joey explained that he saw two girls at the canal
earlier in the day, but that they had left before we
showed up.

"They're teasers," Cory's friend, Jason, said.

I had just remembered his name. His family had
been mentioned in the newspaper when his younger
brother had been kidnapped. Later they found his
body in Kansas, a place, I thought, where only torna-
does ruined people's lives.

Joey and me got to our feet. We climbed on our
bike and said, "See you guys," and pedaled away slowly
through the soft sand. Joey groaned as he tried to pick
up speed. I looked over my shoulder. The two grinning
rhinos were throwing rocks at us. They were not mad
or anything. They just couldn't let us go without doing
something to us. It was in their rhino blood.

We returned to my house, where I fixed us pineapple smoothies. We drank them in a tree and stayed
there until my mother drove up the driveway. She was
with her boyfriend, a guy who looks like a giraffe.

"I'll see you later," Joey said when my mom and her giraffe went inside. He dropped to the ground and rode off. I remained in the tree until it was dusk and the first star appeared in the east. "O star, O star," I sang. "Come back and make me into a boy again. O star, O star, remember when I was in my crib?" I cried a little and then went inside.

The next day Joey showed up doing a wheelie up our driveway. He rode around the lawn standing on the handlebars. Then he jumped from his bike, rolled on the grass, and came up smiling his chimp smile. He had good news.

"I think I got a way to make money."

"Like how?"

Joey brought out a coat hanger from his back pocket.

"Guess?"

Me, I was never good at guessing, even on multiple-choice tests.

"Quit being a chimp!" I growled. "Just tell me!"

Joey raised his eyes up to our roof.

"What does that mean?"

"It means money."

I was tired of Joey playing with me. I posted my long arms on my hips and shook my head, blubbering my lips. I picked up his lowrider bike and held it over my head, threatening to bring it down onto the lawn, hard. I tossed the bike at him. Joey caught it and began to juggle the bike, tire over tire, before he tossed it to me. I juggled it myself and then set the bike down.

"Okay, what do you mean about money?"

Joey explained that because we were good at climbing, we could clean gutters and maybe sweep leaves and stuff off roofs. He said that we could charge, maybe— he used his fingers to make the point—about ten bananas a house.

Because the talk was money, I was all ears. But I blurted out, "Man, it's summer. Ain't no leaves in the gutters."

Joey ignored this technicality. He climbed up our roof and stabbed the coat hanger into the gutter. He held up a bunch of leaves like dollar bills. Joey let the leaves flutter from his hands, and I caught one and turned it over. *Yeah*, I thought. *This could be a money-making scheme.*

We went inside for ice water and halved a greenish banana in partnership.

That afternoon, with me on the handlebars, we pedaled down the street. Joey said that he had a nice uncle who would hire him. His uncle, he related, had only one eye and only one tooth to go with that eye. He said he was really old, something like forty, and had never been married. He'd had a dog once, but the dog went blind in both eyes and had to be put to sleep.

When we arrived in front of Joey's uncle's house, even before we rapped on the front door, we could see that no one was home. The curtains were drawn. Newspapers were piled on the roof. The thirsty flowers in the bed were hanging their heads over.

"When did you last see your uncle?" I asked.

Joey shrugged.

I was reaching for the garden hose to get a drink and to splash the flowers when a neighbor hollered, "What are you two monkeying around in the yard for?"

My hand pulled back from the faucet.

"My uncle lives here," Joey said.

The man sucked on an unlit pipe. "*Did.* He got ill and they had to take him away." The man leaned toward us and, giving off the smell of tobacco, whispered, "They think he has cancer. My name is Melvin."

Joey's mouth dropped into a frown. He fit a finger into his ear and scratched.

"I'm his nephew Joey, and no one told me," Joey said sadly. He pulled his finger out of his ear. Joey pointed at me and introduced me as Ronnie.

The neighbor tapped his pipe against his palm. He jingled his coins and car keys in his pocket.

Seeing the need to move the conversation away from a lull, I announced our entrepreneurial spirit. "Sir, you need your gutters cleaned?" I nudged Joey for him to show the neighbor the coat hanger.

"We call this our gutter wand," Joey explained. He swished it like a sword.

The neighbor frowned. "What are you, a wise guy?"

He narrowed his eyes as if he thought we were making fun of him. He took out his hearing aid, which was the color of earwax, frowned at it, and put it back into the cavern of his old wrinkled ear.

"No, sir, we mean it," I said. I remembered wearing my grandmother's hearing aid at church and thinking that the priest was scolding me. He talked really loud.

"Are you two monkeys?" he asked.

I hated when people finally identified us as the wrong species.

"No, we're chimps," I answered. I was going to explain to him how Joey and me woke up when were thirteen and our bodies had changed. But I figured, why waste our breath on a guy who can't hear?

"Chimps? Monkeys? It's French to me." He asked us how much we would charge to get on the roof and adjust his antenna. "All I get is snowy TV."

Joey gazed at me. I could see dollar signs floating on the lenses of his eyeballs. I could see his lips form the word *Lots.*

"Three dollars," I said.

"Three dollars!"

I argued that it was way up there and that maybe we would get electrocuted rotating the antenna, or that maybe lightning might starch our fur. How would he ever explain to the police about two dead teenage chimps on his roof?

"You got a point there," he said. He licked his lips,

sucked them, and spat them out as if they were an un-flavorful meat. "And I guess you got to figure inflation. Shoot, when I was a kid, I worked all day for three dollars." With a nod, he gave us the go-ahead, hitched up his pants, and went inside.

While we climbed the roof, Melvin opened up the living room window and stuck his head out. "You up there?" he yelled.

"Yeah," I answered.

"YOU UP THERE?" he yelled again.

We remembered that he was hard of hearing.

"YEAH," we hollered in chorus.

Melvin told us to turn the antenna to the left.

Joey and I gripped the antenna, which was hitched up with wires. We muscled our strength together and twisted the antenna until it creaked, from rust. A sparrow settled down to watch our progress.

"Come on! No monkeying around!" Melvin yelled. "I ain't paying you good money for nothing."

Melvin's voice startled the sparrow, which flew away.

"I don't like this guy," Joey said loudly as he scratched his armpits.

I had to agree. But I told him that it was a job and the boss could boss around his workers—or so I had heard. But then I saw that Joey wasn't listening.

"My poor uncle," Joey remarked as he looked over

to his uncle's house. The roof was littered with newspapers.

I told Joey I was sorry that his uncle had only one
eye and hardly any teeth. Plus, cancer?

"I hope I never get sick," Joey said.

"I don't mind getting sick, but losing an eyeball."
I closed an eye and saw the world through one lens. I
didn't like what I saw—everything seemed so far away,
like I was looking through binoculars. I smacked my
lips and imagined eating without any teeth. I could get
soft foods like bananas and oranges down my throat,
but apples and walnuts?

I set my hands on my hips. I turned east, where I
had first seen a star shine down on me and believed
it was God checking out things. This was a god who
didn't care if you changed so much that you were no
longer recognizable from your baby pictures. I told
Joey about the stars and he said, "That's neat."

"Come on!" Melvin hollered again. "*Oprah* starts in
five minutes."

We put our shoulders into our work, a mistake because a wire snapped and struck at us like a snake. The
antenna began to topple slowly.

"Aw, man," I moaned as I skipped back, scared.

The antenna struck the cooler, which sent it off its
foundation and tumbling to the front lawn. We looked
over the edge.

"We didn't mean it, sir," cried Joey. "It was an accident."

We heard the man cuss that he was going to miss *Oprah* and everything else on TV for the rest of the day. We knew enough to climb down off the roof and jump onto Joey's lowrider.

"Go, Joey!" I screamed.

The man appeared at the door, peeling his hearing aid out of his ear. He shoved the hearing aid into his pocket as he ran down the steps. "Stop, you monkeys! Stop right now. Look what you done to my cooler and TV! You're going to pay for this!"

Joey's bike lived up to the words CHIMP POWER pin-striped to the frame. We sped down the block, stopped, and looked back at the calamity that we feared would be our undoing.

"The antenna was real old," Joey reasoned.

"Yeah, it wasn't our fault."

"We risked our lives," Joey said.

I pictured the wire wrapping around our chimp bodies and sending us earthward. I was picturing my own funeral when out of the corner of my eye I caught sight of my mom coming down a set of steps at one pretty house with flowers. Her step was light, full of hope. An Avon bag swung from her shoulders. My mom stopped and, brow furrowed with confusion, looked in our direction.

"I'm busted," I cried.

"No, you ain't," Joey answered. "She's probably thinking that we're monkeys, not chimps. You know how your mom can't see if she ain't got her glasses on."

We rode away, though I thought I could make out Mom yelling, "Chango, is that you?"

At my house Joey and I sat in front of the television, believing that any moment a newsbreak might flash across the screen. "This just in," the announcer would say. "Two teenage chimps cause havoc . . ."

But nothing of the sort happened except that I saw my dad—or at least someone who resembled my dad—in a commercial advertising cheap car tune-ups. The mechanic was leaning over an open hood and striking the engine with a hammer. He was a grease monkey in a gray oil-stained jumper.

"It's my dad!" I said, pointing.

"No way," Joey answered.

The man disappeared from the screen and another man appeared. He pointed at the TV viewer. "You, come on down! We're Tune-Ups for Less. Give us a call right now, and we'll throw in a car wash." The commercial cut to a mechanic beating the engine with a wrench. Two chimps, just like us, were jumping up and down on top of the roof.

"Yeah, man," Joey said, "it looks like your dad all right." He smiled. "And those little dudes look like us when we were littler."

I wagged my head. "Man, my dad's a loser." I got up, went into the kitchen for two apples, and returned to find Joey crying.

"What's wrong?" I asked.

I turned to face the television. Joey had changed the channel to the Animal Planet network.

"They're operating on a gorilla."

A gorilla, with a white cap, was on a table. He was drugged and out of it, though his leg quivered occasionally.

We sat with our apples in our laps. We watched the surgeon, a light attached to his forehead, lower a shiny instrument toward the gorilla's stomach. We winced when the surgeon sawed back and forth.

"I know it hurts," Joey bawled.

We placed our hands first on our eyes, then over our ears. Then, smart me, I turned off the television. The television began to tick as it cooled.

"He'll be okay," I said.

Joey cried with his hands over his eyes.

I tried to cheer him up by juggling little boxes of raisins and by opening the boxes and juggling the raisins themselves. But Joey seemed really down, and I began to think that it had less to do with the gorilla than with our own chimp status.

"I wish I knew where they do Animal Planet," Joey bawled. He cupped his palms, shiny with tears, when I offered him some raisins.

"I know where they make the Animal Planet shows," I lied.

"You don't."

"No, I do." I described a place outside our city, where the animals roamed the fields and hung out in the trees. I said that everyone was nice there. There were no bullies, no mean teachers, no litter, no drive-bys. There was a chimp girl for every chimp boy, and even the rhinos got paired off.

Joey wiped a tear that rolled from his left eye.

I told him about the smoothies that came in buckets and apples big as beach balls. I told him about the sunflowers that dotted the fields, and how you could go up to them and pluck out the seeds if you wanted.

"Is it far away?" Joey asked.

"Nah, not really," I answered. "But you have to go by boat."

"We ain't got a boat," Joey scolded.

"Nah, but we got an inner tube." I described the one hanging in my garage. I told him we should go and check out the location where they shoot for Animal Planet.

"I don't believe you," Joey said. He played with his fingers as he muttered something I couldn't understand but sounded like a prayer. Then he agreed, "Let's go anyhow."

I hurried to the garage for the inner tube, which was flat. I called to Joey, "Hey, come out and help me!"

With Joey on one side and me on the other, we gripped the bike pump and jumped up and down until the inner tube grew as tall as King Kong, our big relative who could handle himself against all other beasts. We rolled it down the driveway just as my mom was coming up the driveway. She honked at us, but we ignored her. She honked a second time.

"Where you going?" she shouted. Her giraffe boyfriend was sitting next to her. His head was sticking out of the sunroof.

"Animal Planet!" I yelled.

We rolled the inner tube to the canal, where we set it on the water.

"You first," Joey said, shivering.

Joey didn't like water, and I didn't like it much, either. But I liked traveling, and with a stick for a paddle I figured we could get far away from our summertime loneliness, even if it was only for a few hours. We couldn't find ourselves chimp girlfriends and had failed in making money at cleaning gutters. I pictured Melvin hauling his cooler back up onto his roof. I pictured him watching a snowy television all through the night.

"Come on," I begged Joey. "Don't be a scaredy-cat."

Joey got into the inner tube, his feet in the doughnut hole. I hopped in next and pushed away from the bank. We drifted to the center of the canal, and soon

the current moved us slowly eastward. I paddled and
kicked my feet occasionally, but mostly the inner tube
moved under its own power. We traveled for a mile
down the canal, and when we saw two teenage burros,
I told Joey that we were getting closer. The two donkey boys were sucking on stalks of grass, and they had
the look of two boys who would work all their lives for
hay and carrots and nothing more.

Joey laughed. "You're lying. We ain't getting close
to Animal Planet. I don't care, either." His smile said
that he was feeling better.

"But we are!" I laughed.

We drifted quietly. I pointed to a eucalyptus with
a pair of owls staring down at us. Leaves followed
the current, and shadows, too. I pointed out how the
fish seemed healthier and not like the ones we'd seen
throwing up what they ate.

It was all made up, but I didn't care. I was with
Joey, my best friend. At dusk I pointed out the first
stars. I started to tell him about the star I had seen from
my crib, but Joey said, "I heard that one already." Then
he said he was sorry and that he would like to hear
about it again. I paddled our inner tube, and sometimes reached up to touch the leaves that hung from
the branches. I stripped some of those leaves and set
them like canoes on the water.

So I began again. I said that when I was a baby,
I spent a lot of time in my crib. There I would think

about the past—like when I first peeled my booties off
my feet and how I once threw my blanket out of the
crib, an act that made me feel guilty for years. I said
that one night a star appeared and winked at me. It
winked actually three times, a sign that in the end I
would be okay but for a long time I would suffer because of family, friends, and school. I would really suffer when I turned into a chimp—that is what the star
told me. But then, in time, I would be okay again. Every mean person I knew would go away. And I would
discover a really good friend.

"That's me, huh?" Joey said.

"That's right—it's you, Joey."

I steered the inner tube back into the middle of the
canal. I continued my story of the star that would guide
us. Right then I realized that the light on the water was
the light of a star that had been racing to reach us for
a long, long time. It was reaching us chimp boys, two
friends with hardly any looks. We were being saved
by a god that was like no other god, but a cool silvery
light.

"You see what I see?" I asked Joey.

"What?" Joey asked.

I pointed.

Joey stared at the water. He appeared confused and
then his face brightened. "It's the star, huh?" He raised
his head skyward.

"O star, O star," I sang.

Joey joined in, kicking his feet from happiness.

"O star, O star," we sang in the early dusk.

So I paddled our inner tube. The current was slow, but we were getting there all the same by the shiny light on a dark and cold canal.

The Sounds of the House

Three days after Maria's mother was buried, the house began to creak and moan, even without the shudder of wind or her father's late-night footsteps to the bathroom. In her bed, which she shared with Angela, her six-year-old sister, Maria could make out those sounds. She believed that they were telling her something—*creak* from their small living room, *moan* in the faraway bathroom. "Is that Mama?" she asked herself. "What does she want?"

Maria listened with the covers to her throat. She listened and then stopped listening when a horn of moon glared through her window, splashing the bed with moonlight the color of spoons. She propped herself up on an elbow and watched the moon tugging along a few stars. "The moon is far away," she lamented, "and so is Mother."

She fell asleep only after the moon moved west and her bedroom darkened. The next morning Maria rose from her bed without disturbing Angela, who lay on her hip, gnashing her teeth in sleep. Her father was at the kitchen table, his face gray in the early morning light. He was drinking coffee, a pile of papers in front of him.

"*Buenos días*," Maria said, almost in a whisper.

When he raised his head and saw Maria, he opened his arms and beckoned her. She approached her father slowly and let her body fall into his arms. She could smell his cologne and the work of cement in his clothes. She could smell his sadness.

She pushed away and ironed down his hair with the flat of her hand. "Papi, you look sleepy," she said softly. "You need a shave."

"*Tired*, not sleepy, *mi'ja*." He rubbed his chin and remarked with a lightness in his voice, "I might grow me a *bigote*."

"Do you want something to eat?" Maria asked as she gazed over her shoulder at the refrigerator. Maria was thirteen, a good cook for a seventh grader, and felt that she should be more responsible.

He ran a hand across his face and, lips pursed, wagged his head. But he raised his coffee cup, which Maria took. While she stood at the stove and reheated the coffee, she looked up at her mother's coffee mug, which hung on a hook under the cupboard. Maria thought of taking it down, but instead she took another cup, her own, and poured herself coffee, which her mother had forbidden her to drink.

"Are you going to work today?" Maria asked as she handed her father his coffee. He had stayed home for a week and was restless to get out of the house. It was late spring, and the lawns were deep green and scraggly from months of winter rains.

He blew on the coffee—blew three times and sipped from the edge cautiously.

"*Sí,*" he answered. "It's better that I work, that I forget." He looked up with the twilight of sadness in his eyes and sighed. "Your mother was a good person—"

"I know," Maria said, cutting him off gently before he got started on the story of their lives.

Feeling sorry for him, for herself, she sat down next to her father and looked at the papers in front of him. They were filled with doodling for a paving job.

"Your math is wrong, Papi," she said after she had inspected his figures. "*Mira.*"

"*¿Qué?*"

"It should be three hundred, not two hundred. You forgot the one."

She pointed a finger at his math, and her father, squinting over the pages, said in a laughing voice, "I've been cheating myself all my life, *mi'ja*. That's why we can't get ahead."

Maria was fixing the math for him when she heard a creak. She cocked an ear and listened. The creak sounded again, this time louder. She let out a squeak and let the pencil jump from her fingers when she heard yet another creak and the scraping of a chair.

"¿Qué pasó?" her father asked.

"Did you hear that?"

Her father raised his head and looked around. "No," he said after a moment of thought, *"No oí nada."*

The door just then swung open to reveal Angela, her little sister, who stood sleepily with a stuffed whale pinched under her arm. She said, "I don't want cereal for breakfast. I want pancakes." Her lower lip pouted.

Since their mother's death, Angela had been acting spoiled and would throw a tantrum at the least provocation. And in the past week she had gotten all kinds of toys, including Rollerblades and a three-ring swimming pool that they had inflated with an air pump. When she became bossy, their father let her have her way. He was sad and troubled by the accident. Their car's front left tire, a retread, had blown on a country road, and the car careened not toward a bush or harmlessly into an empty field but toward an orange tree anchored into the valley earth.

"We have Cap'n Crunch," Maria said.

"No, I want waffles," Angela said. She crossed her arms over her chest. "And hot chocolate."

"How about hot chocolate first?" Maria asked.

Angela's arms fell from her chest. She nodded.

As Angela crawled into her father's lap, thumb in her mouth, Maria went to the refrigerator and brought out a carton of milk. She splashed a cupful of milk into a saucepan and then heaped three spoonfuls of chocolate into a cup.

Angela looked over at Maria, who was watching the milk come to a hissing boil. "I want to use Mommy's cup," she snapped.

"It's Mama's cup, Angela."

"I want to use her cup!"

"Stop it! Quit acting like that!"

"Mommy's dead! She don't care!"

"¡Cállate!" their father cried angrily, turning Angela toward him and shaking his daughter so that the stuffed whale fell from her arms. Angela began to cry and wiggle from his arms. She collapsed to the floor, a bundle of grief.

Their father sighed and picked up his daughter, cooing his *Sorry*s into her hair.

"Okay, you baby," Maria said, a frown on her face, and took the cup from the hook. When she turned over the cup, she discovered a smear of lipstick on the rim. She crossed herself and muttered *"Ay, Dios"* under her breath, a zipper of fear riding up her back.

Maria fixed her little sister her chocolate and then brought out frozen waffles from the freezer. She dropped two waffles into the toaster and looked inside the toaster at the fiery filaments. She thought, *Hell's like that—all red and hot.* When the waffles popped up, Maria stabbed them with a fork and set them on a plate. She laced the waffles with syrup and left the kitchen in a hurry.

"*¿Qué pasa?*" her father called as he looked up from his newspaper. His eyes were the color of newsprint, and as small as the letters he was reading. "What's wrong, Maria?"

"Nothing," she answered. She ran to her bedroom and closed the door. She sat on her bed, with her knees to her chest and cuddling herself. She tried to warm her body that had grown cold with fear as she remembered her mother's words: "*Mi'ja,* I will never leave you. I will always be with you." She rolled over onto her stomach, buried her face in her soft blankets, and started crying. But she stopped crying when she heard a crinkling sound, like the sound of paper being crushed into a ball. *Is it Mother?* she wondered. *Has she come back?* She turned and looked through her tears, scooting into the corner of the bed in fear.

It was her kitten walking on her homework on her desk.

She wiped her eyes and muttered, "You stupid thing. You scared me!" She flung a sock at the cat. It meowed and jumped from the desk, begging for attention. The cat leaped onto the bed, and Maria took it into her arms.

"Are you sad?" Maria asked the cat. "We never got to say good-bye to Mommy."

"Maria, *ven acá*!" Maria heard her father call from the living room. She could hear his heavy work boots ringing on the floor. She pushed the cat aside and jumped off her bed. Angela came into the bedroom. She was sipping from their mother's coffee cup, a mustache of chocolate staining her upper lip.

"I want some more," Angela said, holding up the cup like a chalice.

Ignoring her sister, Maria slipped on a sweatshirt, combed her hair in big long rips, and stomped out of the room with Angela trailing behind, begging for more than chocolate.

"I want some more," Angela whined.

"All right!" Maria yelled as she stopped and wheeled around, hair whipping her shoulders. She hesitated at first in taking the cup from Angela, but finally reached for it. She weighed it in her palm like an orange, thinking that it would weigh no more than a feather. But it was heavy as stone.

"*Me voy*—I'm off," her father told them. His face was shaved and his hair slicked back. "I want you two to stay home today. Tomorrow you can go to school." He gave them each a hug, squeezing love from their small bodies and whispering that they should be good. He gave them each a stick of chewing gum and trudged to the front door, swinging his heavy black lunch pail. The screen door slammed and he was gone.

Maria looked down at the cup in her hand, then at her sister, who was scratching a mosquito bite on her thigh.

"What's wrong?" Maria asked.

"It hurts."

"Put some spit on it."

Leaving her to scratch her bites, Maria went off to the kitchen to fix her sister another cup of hot chocolate. *I should be good to my little brat sister,* she figured. *It'll make Papi happy.*

As she was pouring the steaming milk into the cup, Maria noticed a new smear of red lipstick on the cup. "It's Mom," she whispered to herself, and gazed around the kitchen. Her eyes came to rest on the table, where her mother would sit in solitude admiring her backyard and its flush of flowers. "Mom!" she called in the direction of the table. "Mom, you can't come back!"

There was no answer, no sign, other than the kitchen faucet dripping and a fly beating on the windowsill.

"Mom, are you really here?" Maria asked in a hollow voice. She pounded the table with her fist, and the salt shaker fell over, raining grains of salt.

Angela came into the kitchen. "Who are you talking to?" she asked. "Did Papi come back?"

Maria didn't answer. She stared tenderly at her sister and for a moment thought of hugging her. Instead, she pointed vaguely at the cup of hot chocolate and told her, "It's hot. Be careful not to burn your lips."

Angela picked up the steaming cup of hot chocolate. Turning it around in her small hands and examining it, she asked with a smirk on her face, "Have you been using Mama's lipstick?"

"No," Maria said.

"The cup is all red."

"I didn't use her lipstick. Now, quit it!"

Maria left the kitchen and hurried outside, letting the screen door slam behind her. The sun was dime bright and hot for early May. The sky was blue and marked with a cargo of white clouds in the east. Mexican music drifted over the fence from Señor Cisneros's yard.

Maria climbed onto the tire swing that hung from the mulberry and rocked it slowly, her shoes dragging and scraping the dirt under the swing. *Why?* she thought. *Why has Mom come back?* She remembered an argument they had had the day before she died, an argument about Javier, a boy she liked, a boy with green eyes who was always phoning her. Maria bit her lower lip and felt bad about having snapped at her mother.

She looked at their house, which was pink stucco with a runner of green AstroTurf. Mama hated the fake grass but her father said it wore well, longer than a straw welcome mat.

"Hi!" Angela called from the side of the house. She was holding the coffee cup.

Maria looked over her shoulder. She got off the swing and approached her sister.

"You're not done with your chocolate?"

Angela took a sip and smacked her lips, trying to annoy her older sister. "It tastes good."

Maria noticed that Angela's lips were red. She took Angela's chin roughly into her hands and examined her mouth. "Are you wearing Mom's lipstick?"

"No," Angela answered, pushing away hard and almost losing her balance and falling. Some of the chocolate spilled on the front of her blouse. Mad, Angela looked down at the stain. "See what you've done, stupid!"

"It's nothing. And don't call me stupid."

"I'm going to tell Papi when he comes home," she cried, and stomped off, careful not to spill her remaining hot chocolate.

Maria sat down on the front steps, raking her hand across the AstroTurf. She thought of her mother, gone eight days. *What does she want?* she thought to herself. *Should I be nice to Angela? Should I take care of the house? Of Dad?* Mom had never demanded much, but maybe she was asking for something now.

When a sparrow swooped and settled on the hand-rail, Maria jumped to her feet and cried, *"Ay, Dios."* To her the bird appeared to be the messenger of death. "What do you want? Get outta here!"

The sparrow locked a gaze on Maria, and after a moment of silence flew to the neighbor's roof, then over the house.

Shaken, Maria returned inside the house. Angela, who was in the living room watching television, made a face and said, "I'm gonna tell Papi on you for dirtying my blouse." She muttered under her breath, "Stupid."

Maria passed her without saying anything and went into the kitchen. She looked around slowly as she listened for sounds. The faucet still dripped and the fly now buzzed the overhead light. A ceiling beam creaked, the floor creaked. The water heater in the closet popped and hissed, and the clock on the wall whined its seconds.

"It's Mother," she told herself. "She's telling me something." Maria's gaze fell on her mother's coffee cup on the counter. She walked over and took the cup and poured herself some coffee. She stirred in two spoonfuls of sugar and a splash of milk, and sat down at the small table near the window, her mother's favorite place in the house. She gazed out the window at her mother's garden of tomatoes and chilies, sun-sparking pie tins tied to the vines and banging softly in the breeze.

"What do you want, Mama?" she said after a chill touched her shoulder. "Are you here, Mama? Are you?"

The floor creaked, the ceiling creaked, and the fly that had been buzzing the overhead light beat against the window.

Maria sighed and lowered her gaze on the steam rising from the coffee. She turned the coffee cup around and studied the lipstick marks. She blew on the coffee, raised the cup, and took a sip where the lipstick marks would match her own mouth. Without intending to, she moaned in a different voice, her mother's voice, "I'm here and will never leave you, *mi'ja.*"

Angela was at the dining table drawing a picture with crayons. She asked, "What did you say?"

Maria moaned.

"You sound like Mommy," Angela said. She scratched her thigh, swollen with mosquito bites. With her face scrunched up from the pain of scratching, she asked, "How come you got your hands on your mouth?"

Maria's hands tightened around her mouth as words tried to force themselves from the back of her throat.

"See," Angela said, getting down from the chair. "It's a picture of Mommy." Angela raised the picture

for her sister to see—a picture of the sisters waving to
their mother. In the drawing their mother was calling,
"I'll never leave you, *mi'jas.*"

Maria's mouth twisted with fear. Unable to stop the
words, she let her hands flop at her sides and let their
mother have her say. Their mother's spirit was circling
the house, their lives, with a last good-bye.

One Last Kiss

Daniel Rubio lowered the morning newspaper, stared at the muted television showing a monster truck climbing onto the back of a VW Beetle, and then lifted the newspaper back toward his face. His mouth hung open like a sack as he stared at columns and columns of fugitives wanted by the Fresno Police Department. Each one had a photograph and a description of the crime. They were wanted for burglary, passing bad checks, domestic violence, probation violations, grand theft auto, assault with deadly weapons, attempted murder, and in one case, animal cruelty toward a Chihuahua. Most of the faces—all of them, in fact, except one—looked like those of people who should be taken off the street. The photo of Daniel's grandmother Graciela stared at him with what looked like a smirk. The smirk was saying, "Okay, catch me."

"Dang," Daniel whispered. "Grandma got capped." His grandmother was wanted for passing bad checks. That totally surprised him because Grandma drove a newish car and wore nice clothes. Plus, she smelled of the products she sold—perfume and lotions that promised to rejuvenate aging skin. The lines on her face were filled in with her products, and her lips were red from them, too. Her hair was always in place, and she was a generous grandmother who quickly dispensed her butterscotch Life Savers when she came over to visit.

"Why would she pass bad checks?" he asked himself. Her purse was large as a shopping bag. *She's got to have money in one of those zippered pockets,* he figured. There was a roll of fat on her stomach and hips from all the good eating she'd done. Didn't that prove she was doing okay in life?

"Dang!" he repeated.

Daniel zapped off the television. He set the newspaper aside, stood up, and gazed absently out the window—the winter sky was gray with valley fog. Then he knew why his mother had left early in the morning: She had driven over to her mother's house, his grandmother's house, to see about her problem.

Daniel felt sad as his shoulders sagged. His father had moved out on them two years before and he hadn't come around once, though Daniel had seen him with a woman in the parking lot at Longs Drugs. His father had been holding a heart-shaped balloon in one hand and pushing a stroller with the other. Daniel was angry with his father. When had he ever given his mother a balloon? And that ugly *mocoso* baby! Now this—his grandmother's face in the newspaper.

Daniel sighed as he headed to the bathroom to take an afternoon shower. He was going to the junior high dance, though he didn't know how to dance and had to admit to himself that he wasn't good-looking. Even if he knew how to dance, where would he get the strength in his voice to ask, "Hey, girl, you wanna dance?" Or some other bold line, like, "*Ruca*, I'm for real!"

"I can't believe it! Grandma!" he shouted in the shower. His face was bearded with foaming bath gel and his eyes stung from the shampoo, two products that his grandmother had sold him. When he had bought them from her, Daniel had suspected that they had already been opened, but he feared saying anything because his mother would find out and lower the boom on him. Plus, he would have felt awkward telling his grandmother, "Looks like someone used them already."

He dressed and cooked himself an egg burrito laced with strips of baloney. He ate staring at the turned-off television, his hand within inches of the newspaper that carried the picture of his grandmother. He almost cried, and not as the result of eating his burrito in five big chomps. It was because of the newspaper photo. He muttered, "We're messed up."

He was thinking of his family. His mother was a single mother, and his older sister, Rebecca, at nineteen, was a single mother, too. His sister lived in Merced, an hour's drive away, where she worked at a swap meet, selling stuffed animals and plastic toys that fell apart after one use.

"Wonder where Mom is," he said vaguely after a while. He was going to ask her for ten dollars for the dance. He was also going to ask her for a ride. He washed his plate and frying pan, and then tidied up the living room. While he was finishing that little chore, the telephone rang.

"Yeah," he answered on the fourth ring.

"Mi'jo," a voice whispered.

It was his grandmother Graciela.

"Grandma? Where are you?" He held back his tongue, which nearly let loose that he had seen her picture in the *Fresno Bee.*

His grandmother ignored the question. She told him to tell his mother that she had forgotten her cell phone at her house. She was using it at that moment but wasn't home. Grandma then asked, *"Mi'jo,* what do you want for Christmas?"

A supply of good looks, he considered bargaining for.

Instead, he answered truthfully, "I want you with us. Maybe we can make tamales."

"You said the ones in the cans are better," his grandmother threw at him. There was a touch of anger in her voice.

"Nah, Grandma. That was a joke." He laughed a little to show that he had been kidding.

The reception of the cell phone faded and cracked, and then the phone went dead after a series of clicks.

At five-thirty he wrote a note to his mother saying that he was off to the dance and would return home at ten, eleven at the latest. He said he had taken three dollars from the cupboard and promised to return the money when he could. From his sock drawer he fumbled for the two dollars he kept there and then for extra luck sprayed his throat with the cologne his grandmother had sold him. But he had to wonder what girl would sniff around his throat—*No girl.*

He pedaled his bike against a chilly wind to his best friend Vince Torres's house, a mile away and down a street that was dark as a tunnel—the streetlights were busted out and the porch lights off. Darkness had grown thick and the fog cold. By the time he arrived at Vince's house, his nose was running. His ears were red and his eyes were watery.

"Hey, homes," Vince barked through the curtain before Daniel even knocked. "Just leave your bike on the porch—it'll be okay."

"Yeah, like stolen, *ese*," Daniel countered. He guided his bike to Vince's backyard and chained it to their clothesline. Daniel wiped the soles of his shoes and invited himself through the back door and into the kitchen, where Vince's mother looked up and slowly let a frown pull down her already sagging face.

"Oh, Danny, I saw—" she started as she spread her arms and welcomed Daniel into their stringy warmth.

So she knows, Daniel thought. She would have to know because Daniel's grandmother had sold her cologne, too, or had it been the three shades of lipstick called Mood Changes? Still, he didn't walk into this woman's arms. No, he remained near the back door, looked over her shoulder, and called, "Hey, Vince— ready? *¿Listo?*" He wanted to get away from his best friend's mother, who appeared to be wringing her hands for information. When it wasn't forthcoming, she announced, "She'll be okay. You wait and see." Then in a whisper flavored with the cheese she had been cutting at the kitchen counter, she said, "Vince doesn't know. How is your mother?"

"She ain't home," Daniel admitted.

"Your mother is with your grandmother, huh?" Vince's mother's eyes were wet with excitement. Her hands were held high, resembling the crippled arms of a praying mantis.

Daniel turned away without answering and exited through the back door, ignoring her pleas to come back and have some hot chocolate. "Mom's right—the woman's a *chismosa*." He felt like unlocking his bike and returning home to mope in front of the television. He would have except Vince bounced down the back steps and growled, "Look at the money I got."

Daniel released the bike chain. He admired the two twenties in Vince's palms. He also admired his friend, who was better looking than him and slimmer. His teeth were straight, not like the car wreckage in Daniel's own mouth.

The two twenties disappeared from his hands like a magic trick, and the smile on his face collapsed. Vince was suddenly all business. "Let's see if we can get us some girls."

Vince was confronted by a girl who stomped her dainty feet, propped her hands on her hips, and screamed above the music, "Me first!" The girl had purple streaks in her hair and a tattoo of a bunny on her forearm. The bunny was playing air guitar.

"Slow down, girl," Vince said, a playful smile working its magic from the corner of his mouth.

But she didn't slow down. She pressed up against Vince, inhaled the air around him, and cooed, "You smell good." She sniffed Vince's neck, and Vince opened his collar, where she planted a quick kiss. She dragged him onto the basketball court, which had been turned into a dance floor. Daniel swallowed and discovered a lump of jealousy forming in his throat. He stepped away from the crowd of dancers jumping to the throbbing music.

"Vince gets them all," Daniel remarked. He then bumped against someone whose smile deflated into a sneer and who said, "You better not step on my shoes."

"Sorry," Daniel apologized hurriedly.

"You got that right," the kid snarled. The kid's face was a dartboard of pimples. He was smaller than Daniel, but his ropy arms were lean with muscle. His right eye was flecked with the blood of anger inside him. Daniel had never seen him before, but the sneering face was backed up by dudes he knew—one was a guy with whom he had shared sandwiches in elementary school. Since then they had shared nothing except the heartache of attending a school etched with graffiti and littered with hamburger wrappers and paper cups.

Daniel moved away. He felt lonely in spite of the bodies around him. From the corner he watched the dancers and spied the red glow of a lit cigarette. He smelled smoke and remembered the saying, Where there's smoke, there's fire. He waited for the fire of fists or a couple kissing so fiercely that the security guards in windbreakers would have to break them apart. But the cigarette was just sucked until it was dropped and rubbed into the floor.

"I should go home," he told himself. He pictured

his grandmother being led away in handcuffs. Her face was lowered in shame but still dolled up with the products she sold. *Yeah, I should go home,* he thought. *Mom probably needs me.*

His chest rose and produced a sigh. He left the gym, but couldn't force himself to leave just yet. He liked the song the DJ had just pumped up. He stood outside, listening to the song's anthem that you couldn't trust anyone, not even your best friend. "It's true," he vouched. "It's real true. Like my dad! He ain't true." He played in his mind the recurring image of his father walking with that strange woman in the parking lot of Longs Drugs. "I hate him," he spat. "My life is stupid."

He had the evidence that his life was stupid. He was thinking about the cheap necklace his mother had gotten him for Christmas. His mother had carelessly bought a necklace with a charm that was an *O,* instead of a *D* for Daniel. His own mouth had become an *O* when, on his knees, he had unwrapped the gift in front of their Christmas tree. He would have told his mother about her error, but he knew that her mood would sour. She would scold him for being ungrateful.

He next was thinking about his grandmother when he felt a hand on his arm and then a face coming close to his. He wasn't sure what was happening. Was it that dude who had threatened him earlier? Had Vince come out to whisper some naughty detail about the girl he had danced with? Was the face that of a vampire lowering its fangs toward his throat? His speculation stopped there. He felt a pair of lips lower and a slight suctioning of a kiss. The pair of lips brushed his throat.

"I was waiting for you," the girl purred. "You playing hard to get, or what?"

Playing hard to get, he thought as he swallowed. *Never!*

"You're teasing me, huh," the voice said playfully. The girl hugged him around his neck. They kissed again. He tasted the glossy lipstick that smelled like mint. He wanted more, a lot more. He was also happy that he had sweetened his breath earlier with a stick of chewing gum. He was glad to be alive, in the dark, and in the arms of a girl who was warm and generous with her praise.

"Where were you?" The girl stomped her foot, and Daniel was surprised that her heels didn't kick up a bushel of sparks. By those sparks, perhaps, he could have made out her face. Then again, she would have made out his and immediately run away. He would have considered it love at first sight except that he couldn't really make out her face. He could make out a pout and the gleam of three studs in her left earlobe.

"You were waiting for me?" he asked meekly. He pointed a finger at his heart.

The girl let out a sharp cry when she realized her mistake. She had kissed not her intended lover boy but a stranger. She let out another cry, turned, and ran away, leaving Daniel raising his right hand and asking—begging, he would later confess to himself—for her to come back.

The girl disappeared into the gym.

"Dang," he muttered. He sucked in his breath and could feel the cool minty taste on his lips. He repeated that action and was dizzy with wonder. It was a fresh experience, a kiss that made him breathless. He then admonished himself.

"She's gone, dawg!" He scolded his lazy soul for not acting quicker. He lowered his face and bit a knuckle. Who was she? He was excited, as this was the first time he had ever been kissed. He liked it—he liked it a lot— and now she was gone.

He hurried back into the gym, where the music had suddenly stopped. The principal, Mr. Warden, his tie undone, was spitting threats into the microphone as he foretold the future. He said he was going to stop the dance if he caught one more student smoking.

"DO YOU UNDERSTAND ME?" he barked. A vein on his neck stood out, and his eyes were wide with fury. That his own breath smelled of cigarettes was beyond the point.

There were a few yeahs, but most of the students looked down at their shuffling shoes. Some muttered snide threats; others were searching through pockets for chewing gum to cover up their cigarette breath. Mr. Warden was known to come up to students and sniff their breath, all the while rolling an Altoid in his mouth.

Mr. Warden finished ranting. The music came on with a blare, and a few dancers took to the floor, though their bodies were moving slow and cautiously. Most hung on the side, in rebellion against Mr. Warden and some of the parent chaperones who were policing the students.

Daniel watched the female dancers. *Is that her?* he wondered. *Or her over there? Maybe that's the one.* His attention settled on a girl standing alone, one leg crossed over the other, her thumbs hooked in her pants pockets. He walked past her, his eyes slicing a quick look to see if her mouth was shiny with lip gloss and if her earlobe held three studs.

Nah, he concluded. She had a single dangling earring, not three studs, and her lips were red, and what he had tasted was a clear lip gloss, that much he knew. Plus, she was tall, and the girl that he had held briefly in his arms was an inch or two shorter than him.

Daniel circled the gym, sizing up the girls but turning away quickly when one of them caught his eye. He didn't want to appear desperate, but he admitted that he was. He felt like a werewolf in search of a lover baby.

He noticed his friend Vince was munching a Life Saver, and Daniel guessed that he had been one of those sucking cigarettes. He started to walk toward the group that Vince was with.

But Vince looked right through him, a sign that he didn't want Daniel to come near. He was hanging with other people, at least for that night, who were a notch or two up on the social ladder.

"You're a stupid snob," Daniel cursed under his breath.

Toward ten o'clock Daniel felt even more desperate as some of the students were beginning to leave.

"She's gotta be here," he whined to himself. He then rocked on the heels of his shoes as he made out a girl with three studs in her earlobe. She was holding a guy's hand and they were headed toward the door. Daniel followed, but not too closely. He made his way bumping among others who were leaving, trailing the girl and the guy she was with.

"Dang," he muttered. "She should really be mine."

The night was cold, dark. He saw the couple, cooing like pigeons. They began to kiss.

Daniel swallowed. He tasted envy on his tongue. *It's gotta be her,* he thought.

Her arms wrapped around the boy as they kissed, laughed, and kissed again. Then she pushed him away to scream playfully, "No!"

Daniel could have wept. It was the most tender no

he had ever heard. Usually when his mother said no, it sounded like gunshot. When teachers said it, it was a door slamming closed by an angry wind.

When the boy and girl began to kiss again, Daniel turned and walked away, disturbed because the girl was no longer saying no but a repeated yes. He was weak from jealousy. "Why can't it be me?" he whimpered. "I never get anything good." He dragged his body away from the love scene.

When he got home he was greeted by his mother screaming from the kitchen, "Where have you been? Did you wipe your feet?" He pictured her at the stove, rubbing her hands over the burners. He pictured his mother dipping her hands into the blossomlike fire; she could take a lot of punishment.

Daniel sighed, and with the sigh something like hope was released from his lungs. He swiveled his head to the right and was only mildly surprised to see his grandmother asleep on the couch, her mouth open. A faint gargle issued up with each exhale of breath. He'd had a suspicion that when he came home, his grandmother would be there. And there she was, snoring ungraciously under the glare of an end lamp. Her veined hands were gripping the crumpled section of the newspaper in which her name and face appeared.

"I was at the dance," he told his mother. "And yeah, I wiped my feet," he lied.

"You better," his mother said. Her face was smeared

with night cream. Some of it was clotted in her bangs. Her eyes were raw-looking against the rest of her face. She looked like a clown but was anything but funny.

"I was at the dance," he repeated, and plucked a potato chip from the bowl on the kitchen counter. "You said I could go. Didn't you get my message?"

His mother was stirring a cup of dark tea. She raised it to her face, and when she sipped, the night cream around her mouth began to crack, showing fissures. She sipped two more times before she said, "Your grandmother is in trouble."

Daniel stopped rolling his tongue over his back molars. He stared at the calendar on the refrigerator, stared in that direction because he couldn't look at his mother. He waited for her to add more. He dropped another potato chip into his mouth.

"The police are going to come for her," she stated coldly. Her face tilted upward to the clock on the wall. "It's ten-thirty, and they said they should be here by eleven." Suddenly tears leaked from his mother's face. The tears cut grooves and melted some of the night cream on her cheeks.

"I know," Daniel said.

"What do you know? You don't know nothing!"

With that burst of anger, Daniel made his escape to his bedroom, where he threw himself on his unmade bed. "She's so mean," he muttered about his mother, whose footsteps he heard propelling her toward the bathroom. He heard the groan of plumbing in the wall—his mother must have been washing off her night cream.

"My life is stupid," he moaned. He tried with all his might to re-create the kiss he had experienced only a few hours before. He saw a girl's face raise toward his. He puckered up his lips, and then parted them as he recalled that was how he had caught the kiss of that strange unknown girl. He licked his lips, but the minty taste of lip gloss was gone. He turned onto his elbow and squeezed his pillow. *Who is she?* he wondered. *Who? Who? Who?*

There was a knock on his door, followed by a shout. "You better get up and say good-bye, Mr. Know-It-All!"

"I'm not Mr. Know-It-All!" he screamed back.

To his surprise his mother didn't come down on him with her usual fist-clenching threats. He pushed himself up from his bed. His grandmother was headed for a night in jail, possibly longer if it was true that she had been passing bad checks.

"Mi'jo!" Daniel's grandmother called while dabbing on lipstick in front of the small mirror in the dining room. She turned after she had finished and said, "They said I did it, but I didn't do it." She pouted, as she expected her grandson to come to her defense.

Daniel only stared at his grandmother.

Suddenly they heard a car stop in front of the

house. Two doors opened and closed, one clicking closed softer than the other.

Daniel's mother began to cry and heave her shoulders in an eruption of emotion that he had never witnessed before. He watched his mother hug his grandmother, saying, "Mom, don't worry. You're going to be out tomorrow. I'll call Junior."

Junior was his mother's half brother.

Mother and daughter hugged and kissed. Daniel could only watch and pushed back into his mind the awful thought that maybe his grandmother was guilty and deserved to be led away.

His mother and grandmother parted but held hands, both sniffling and allowing tears to run down their faces. It was, Daniel thought, a race of tears—he noticed that the long teary trail was longer on his mother's face than on his grandmother's.

She really did it, he concluded. *She really passed bad checks.*

When a knock rapped at the door, mother and daughter let go of each other.

Grandmother turned to her grandson. "I'm going now," she said with a sniffle. Her eyes were moist with tears, her face long from the gravity called age.

"Don't just stand there! Give your grandmother a kiss good-bye!" his mother scolded.

Daniel stepped obediently toward his grandmother and spread his arms. He held her for a few seconds, and for half of those seconds he thought of the girl outside the gym. That was the first girl he had ever kissed, and the kiss had come unexpectedly. He realized there would be other times when he might duplicate such happiness. In his grandmother's arms, it was not one of those times.

They parted.

"You be good," his grandmother instructed. "I didn't do it. That man is a liar."

"I know you didn't," Daniel lied.

"This man turned me in, *mi'jo*, because I don't like him. He's married and that's why I don't like him."

"I know," Daniel found himself saying as she confessed that she had liked the man—*Who was he?*—for a month and then stopped returning his calls.

Daniel's mother stomped to the front door when the knock sounded again, harder.

"All right! All right already!" his mother snarled. She squeegeed tears from her face with her thumb. She primped her hair.

His grandmother quickly gave Daniel a kiss on the cheek, which seemed to burn. He touched that cheek and offered up a remote "Bye, Grandma."

His grandmother turned and hurried to the front door, where she hugged her daughter one last time and closed the door behind her.

Daniel's mother sat on the couch, lowered her face into her palms, and sobbed. He considered sitting next

to his mother to comfort her but decided he should
return to his bedroom. There he sat on the edge of
his bed but couldn't locate the tears inside himself to
cry for his grandmother. "What's wrong with me?"
he asked himself. "You're cold! You can't even cry for
your grandmother. You're hateful! Hateful! Hateful."

But he sensed it was an untrue outburst. It was
something to say at a moment when he should have
been crying. He stood up and looked in the mirror. He
touched his hot cheek and realized there were different
kinds of kisses—sweet and mysterious ones like from
the girl who suctioned his breath outside the school
gym. Then there were kisses—he swallowed hard and
turned away from the mirror—like those from his
grandmother, one that left a red lipstick stain like a
small bloody wound.

Raiders Nation

Adan's father, Ramiro Islas, was born in Del Rey, California, on a Sunday in March when his town of nine hundred had experienced an unexpected blessing. A wind had snapped through the valley and shook a flurry of blossoms from the plum and almond trees that circled the town. Some said the blossoms covered the street like snow. They whitened lawns and cars parked in driveways and sent children, arms flapping like wings, outside to catch them in their mouths. It was certain that the blossoms that covered the ground were responsible for Doña Lilia Marquez slipping and wrenching not only her two knees but also her back. She had complained about it that day and up till the hour of her death.

That had been thirty-two years ago, when Ramiro was brought into the world on a quiet day. He was quiet, too, all his life. His family was surprised, then, when he fell in love. He married Gloria Mesa, a part-time seamstress who was equally quiet. They ate their meals in silence, or near silence. When he wished to perk up his steak or roast chicken, he would ask, "Salsa and pepper, please," or, in Spanish, *"La salsa y pimienta, mi cielo."* For him, Spanish was softer in tone than guttural-sounding English.

In their third year of marriage, they had a son, whom they named Adan in honor of Ramiro's maternal grandfather. Adan was born unexpectedly at 5:00 P.M. on a Friday. Ramiro's father had said that those born on Sunday, especially in spring, were meant to live quiet lives. Those born on Friday or Saturday would be outgoing and possibly rowdy. Ramiro's own father had been born on a Monday, the first day of the workweek. And work he did, up until the moment he died, falling from a scaffold while painting a house for a friend.

"He looks like you!" Gloria said proudly when she and the baby came home from the hospital. The baby's features were beginning to take shape.

Ramiro agreed that Adan looked like him, but the baby's temperament was nothing like his. Within a week of his birth, Adan was screaming and kicking. Face furrowed from anger, he looked like a little old man in his new blankets. He was hot tempered and stubborn, and was already swinging his fists everywhere.

"He's so loud," Ramiro said. He recalled his father's wisdom about babies born on Friday or Saturday. Maybe they were destined to be rowdy after all.

Gloria could only smile. "He's going to test us, *mi vida.*"

Years passed, and the prophecy came true. Adan did test his parents. His father worked as a security guard at a fruit-processing plant and would sometimes bring home a bag of almonds or dried apricots. Little Adan would make a face and mutter, "Yeah, thanks." His father, in a near hush, would read the comics to little Adan, who after listening would ask, "What's so funny about that?"

"Why is he like this?" the boy's mother would cry. "What did we do?"

Adan began to fight, to tag walls with graffiti, and to use bad language. The family's grief deepened when Adan was caught sifting through boxes in a neighbor's garage. The neighbor had collared the ten-year-old boy and walked him roughly to his father's house. The neighbor pounded on the front door.

"Your boy was in my garage, stealing!" the neighbor had roared.

Ramiro could only blink. He lacked the words to express his disappointment. After all, he was a security guard and had taught and warned his son about gangs and crimes and such. But stealing at such a young age? And from a neighbor?

"You sure?" Ramiro had asked. He had great respect for his neighbor, who was an elder at the Mexican Baptist church. He was a man who kept his house tidy and his lawn mowed and green as money. A ragweed didn't last more than a day in his flower bed. And snails? They marched to their death under his command.

"I'm sure!" the neighbor had roared even louder. He was not a kindly Baptist at that moment. He was a man who expected his neighbor to correct his son.

Gloria had come to the front door. She wrung her hands as her eyes filled and cascaded tears down her face.

"¡Chale! I wasn't stealing nothing!" Adan argued. He shook off the neighbor's hand from his neck. "What you got to steal that I want? You think I want your push mower or your broom? And I saw you got a box of Playboys back there."

The tears on his mother's cheeks dripped like diamonds. Indeed, they were as priceless as her love for her son. Her shoulders began to jerk from a deep and painful crying. "Oh, Adan ... Oh, Adan." That had been two years ago. At twelve, Adan exasperated his parents, who trembled when the telephone rang. They would look at that instrument attached to the kitchen wall. Was it the principal calling once again? A manager from a store, red-faced with anger about their son shoplifting? Or worse, the police? Maybe their son had broken into a house.

Then a marvelous piece of luck happened. Adan was beaten up by an older boy. Adan came home one evening while Ramiro was playing solitaire at the kitchen table and Gloria was balancing the checkbook. He presented his swollen face to his parents. Ramiro let the cards fly into the air, and the pen danced from Gloria's fingers. Their son was wounded! They bathed his face and set ice cubes wrapped in a washcloth onto his swollen jaw. They gently fit cotton balls into his nostrils and wiped blood from behind his ears. Their son had little to say that evening, and the next day after the swelling had subsided, he had even less to say.

"What happened, son?" his father had asked when he returned home from work.

Adan could only say, "I was wrong."

"Who was the boy who did this?" his father asked.

"A friend."

A friend? His father had to wonder what kind of friend beats you up.

"I was a fool, Papi." Adan wept. "I stole some money from my friend." For the first time in years, tears leaked not only from the son's face but also from the father's lined face. Adan leaned his head against his father's shoulder, and that evening father and son became friends.

Not long after that incident, Ramiro realized that he should have spoken up more over the years when his son had been growing up. He should have told him, "No, you can't do that!" Or, "Listen to me! I'm your father." Moreover, he sensed that he should have signed up his son for soccer or Little League Baseball or maybe even football, a sport that made Ramiro squint with pain when he saw teams clashing on television. He didn't care about that rough sport. It was just too loud for him. Occasionally he would catch a glimpse of a football game at his wife's brother's house. He couldn't help it. His brother-in-law had TVs in every room, including—Ramiro was aghast when he first encountered it—the bathroom.

"Adan, we're going to do things together," Ramiro had told his son. He made that promise in September, when the first leaves were falling calmly onto lawns and the pavement. It was football season in a small town. Ramiro signed up Adan for a football league that included mostly religious schools—Baptist, Methodist, and Catholic. He couldn't imagine his son getting hurt on the field. After all, weren't the players the sons of religious people?

Adan was excited, but worried about his jaw, which pained him when he had to speak more than six words in a row. But he made the cut, and soon Adan was stringing six and seven words together without pause. He was on the mend, and his body appeared to change as well. He put on muscle that filled his T-shirts. He could run for miles without breathing hard. He went to practice twice a week, and his father, still dressed in his security guard uniform, would arrive after work to watch his son.

"Don't worry, *mi'jo*," Ramiro said as he helped suit up Adan for the first game. "You have your helmet." Logic had him once again arguing that most of the opponents were Christians and, therefore, not as vicious as teams in nonreligious leagues.

Secretly, before their league's first game, Ramiro had tried on his son's helmet. He looked at himself in the bathroom mirror and bared his teeth. He growled, "I'm like a Chicago Bear," and chuckled to himself.

He drove Adan to the game and sat in the bleachers, where he watched his son, a third-string wide receiver, sit and sit until the coach finally put him in for two plays. Adan ran his routes, but the ball wasn't tossed to him. Then he was taken out, but put back in during the fourth quarter. Ramiro cheered when Adan made a catch and ran twelve yards before he was tackled. He was proud that his son's knees were stained green with grass and that his left elbow was dark with mud.

That night Adan's family feasted on Mexican food— enchiladas, frijoles, and arroz piled tall as the pyramids of Mexico. A fiery salsa brought sheens of sweat to their brows.

"You should have seen our boy," Ramiro bragged to his wife. He described the catch over and over, until his wife, blushing with pride, cried, "Oh, I should have been there!" Tears filled her eyes as she set her fork down and brought her hands together, as if in prayer. She said she was sorry she had missed it. She had stayed home because she didn't want to see her son get hurt.

Adan patted her arm. "There will be other times." He scooped up frijoles in his tortilla and chewed carefully. He admitted to his father that his jaw had been rattled in the game, but it had been his fault. He had forgotten to properly bite down on his mouthpiece.

The next day, a Saturday, Ramiro scanned the newspaper. In the corner of the sports section he saw the Oakland Raiders schedule.

"They're playing the Eagles," he muttered. He wondered who the Eagles were. He scanned all the articles about professional football. They took up almost the entire page. He was amazed.

"Adan," he called. "What does *NFL* mean?"

Adan looked up from his homework. "It means 'National Football League.'"

Ramiro reflected.

"Where do the Eagles play?" he asked.

"Philadelphia," Adan answered.

Philadelphia. Ramiro began to think about professional football teams. He closed his eyes, with the newspaper on his lap, as if he were sleeping, and then got up a few minutes later without his usual groan of tiredness. He sneaked away and got onto the Internet, an elaborate computer maze that his wife had taught him recently. He searched for *NFL*, and was amazed at the sites that were available to investigate. He had to wonder where he had been in recent years. Excited, he looked up the Oakland Raiders, which he decided was his favorite team. He nearly cried when he read about the history of the team—its division championships and its numerous Super Bowls. He then located an Oakland Raiders store, where you could purchase items.

"These are the real things," he whispered.

Ramiro looked over his shoulder. He took out his credit card and nervously typed in the number. He bought an authentic jersey, a small Raiders helmet, and a set of drinking glasses. He reassured himself that he never bought himself anything, and besides, didn't he work hard? Still, he was surprised by his impulse buys—and by the Internet!

When his purchases arrived with a toot from a UPS truck, Ramiro's wife was upset.

"They cost so much!" she cried softly.

"Yes, but they're the real things," he protested. He showed her the inside of the helmet that said: *Authentic Merchandise of the Oakland Raiders.*

Then Ramiro had an accident that he believed was possibly divine providence. While he was pruning a rosebush in the yard, a branch slapped him in the face when he let go. The branch scratched his left eye, causing him to stumble into the house, a cupped hand over his injury. From that day on, his eye teared. His doctor prescribed some drops, but they had no effect. Finally, the doctor gave him an eye patch and ordered him not to drive at night.

His wife cried. Adan dug up the rosebush in anger and tossed it in the compost heap in the corner of the yard. But Ramiro felt completely different about the matter. "I'm a Raider," he announced to the bathroom mirror. He was thinking of the Raiders symbol: a football player with an eye patch. He found himself repeating the Raiders motto: Commitment to Excellence.

At work Ramiro sensed that his coworkers were in awe of his eye patch and the Raiders cap that he sometimes wore backward, like a teenager might. He became an expert on the folklore of the Raiders and knowledgeable about past and present players. During his break and lunchtime, Ramiro would sometimes toss a football with other workers. He surprised himself. He could toss the football with accuracy and with sting.

There was not a week when Ramiro didn't make a Raiders purchase. He was able to keep up his habit because he sold the family's second car, a Toyota with bald tires and a leaky radiator. The car was a piece of junk, he had argued, plus dangerous on the road.

His wife cried one Monday when he came home from work, "Why are you buying so many of these things?"

"Why?" he asked as he put his lunch box down on the kitchen counter. "Because of our son. We need to keep him in football." He asked her if Adan hadn't become a better person since he had joined football.

His wife became quiet as she bowed her head.

Ramiro hugged his wife and said, "He's our only son."

He washed up and sat in his recliner. He fiddled for his pocketknife among the keys and coins in his pocket. He pushed the blade into the flap of a box that had come in the mail and sawed slowly. He brought out a silver and black Raiders lampshade that immediately replaced the fluffy one on the corner lamp.

His wife ran from the living room, crying.

"Gloria, it cost hardly anything!" he yelled. But he had sensed that his purchase—and the other ones—had nothing to do with money. It had to do with change. He shrugged, snuggled into his recliner, and closed his eyes as he waited for six o'clock. The Raiders were playing the Ravens on *Monday Night Football*.

The house became a temple of Raiders mementos—the throw rug, the extra blanket, the mirror, the ashtray they filled with candies wrapped in silver and black cellophane. There was more—jackets and T-shirts, water bottles, and jewelry for his wife. Ramiro hoisted a Raiders Nation flag in front of his house. When lowriders passed by in their tricked-out cars with hydraulics, he would clench his fist and yell, *"Órale, vato!"*

"You shouldn't shout like that!" his wife protested. "What will the neighbors think?"

"But it's for us, baby!" Ramiro answered. He clapped a hand over his mouth. He had never called his wife baby. Where had he learned that? Then he became aware that it was from the personal motto of the owner of the Raiders: Just win, baby. He turned that phrase over in his mind: *Just win, baby.* He liked it. He pulled his wife to his chest and hugged her. In her ear, he whispered, "It's for Adan, for our son."

"What is?" his wife asked as she pushed him away.

"We need to keep him busy," he answered. "To keep him in sports." He didn't have to remind her about their son's behavior.

But Adan became less interested in football when he became a resolution counselor at school. When there was a fight, he tried to make the enemies friends, and he even befriended the boy who had beaten him up. In the school newspaper, he had a weekly column called "La Paz." He answered questions about gangs and teenage issues.

Adan still played football the next season, and joined his dad on Sunday mornings to watch the Raiders games on TV.

"The Raiders are going all the way this year," his father boasted from his recliner. The Raiders blanket draped over his lap and legs hid his Raiders slippers.

"Dad," Adan said one Sunday morning after a large breakfast that had sent his father to the couch to nap before the start of the game. "Dad, you need to stop it."

"Stop what, *mi'jo*?"

"This Raiders thing," Adan answered.

Ramiro sat up and put on his eyeglasses, which were black with a streak of silver.

"Dad, you've changed, and Mom doesn't like it."

Ramiro smiled. "But you and me, we got something."

Adan blinked at his father, confused.

"We got a mission, a purpose." He peered at the Raiders clock on the television. "*Ay*, the game's already started." He reached for the remote control and snapped on the television, then hit the RECORD button. He had stockpiled the last nineteen games of the Raiders.

Adan rose and left his father to his game.

Indeed, Ramiro, who had been born on a quiet Sunday in a quiet town, had changed. He would clench his fists when he saw another car or truck on the road with a Raiders flag attached to the antenna. He would yell, *"Órale, ese!"* And for those who had San Francisco 49er flags? He would shake his head and mutter, *"Estúpido."*

The merchandise continued to arrive—the Raiders car plates, the videos, the books, the calendar, and the cigarette lighter. Ramiro trembled and became speechless when he received a signed photograph of Crystal, a cheerleader. It was signed: *To Ramiro, all my best, XXX, Crystal.*

In the garage, away from his wife, who happened to be peeling potatoes at that moment, he shared the signed photograph with his son.

His son frowned.

"What's wrong? Don't you like her?"

"No," he answered.

Ramiro didn't understand. "Why?"

"Because she's not Mom." He walked away, tall as a soldier.

Because he was in the garage and it was an hour until kickoff time, Ramiro brought out his mower. He completed his weekly task, then took one more longing look at the picture of Crystal before he rolled it up like a treasure map and hid it in the rafters. He hurried into the house. He got himself a soda and fit it into a Raiders cup holder.

Ramiro was happy following the Raiders on television. But not long after he had received the signed photograph, he learned that one of the younger security guards had gone to see the Raiders play the San Diego Chargers. The security guard described the tailgate parties, and the wild outfits of the fans. Ramiro became dreamy. He saw himself there, and not at the fifty-yard line but in the Black Hole, where the rowdiest of fans bellowed, shouted, and showed off their frightful costumes. He saw himself with a small skull on his shoulder, something not too big, because he figured that he was really a newcomer to the Black Hole. He didn't want to show up the veterans. They had earned the right to wear human-sized skulls on their shoulders—plus the chains, breastplates, the helmets— and to have their faces painted silver and black.

"How did you get your ticket?" Ramiro asked the security guard.

"I got mine from a dude I know, but you can also get them on the Internet."

"But I want to sit in the Black Hole." Ramiro knew that such tickets were impossible to get.

The security guard smiled. "I'll fix it up for you."

To Ramiro the young man resembled a smiling skull. He hadn't really liked him before (the man had the habit of cleaning his teeth with a toothpick), but suddenly Ramiro realized how wrong he had been about him. If the tickets came through, he was going to allow the young man to take a peek at the signed photograph of Crystal.

Three days later Ramiro got the tickets, a pricey expenditure but worth it. The Raiders were playing the Denver Broncos, their mortal enemies because of some disputed play from the 1970s. That evening he called Adan into the garage.

"I've already seen her," Adan said angrily.

Ramiro became confused. *"¿Cómo?* What?" Then he realized that his son was talking about the signed photograph of Crystal. "Oh no, Adan. It's even better." He took out his wallet and presented to his son the two tickets.

Adan looked at them, baffled. "Tickets?"

"No, not just tickets. Black Hole tickets." He explained to his son where they would be sitting and among whom. He told him about the fans who wore skulls on their shoulders and painted their faces silver and black.

"I don't want to go!" Adan protested.

"But you have to. You're my son." Ramiro kicked among the boxes in the garage and took out the small skull he intended to mount on his shoulders. "See," he said, and placed it on his left shoulder. The skull was little bigger than a softball, and in its eye sockets glowed luminous green eyes. "Looks nice, huh?"

"Dad, that looks ridiculous! You're too old—" Adan stopped himself.

"Too old, huh? Should I be *un viejo* playing checkers under a tree?" He nearly bit his tongue when he remembered his late father and how the two of them often played checkers under a tree.

"Dad, it just don't seem right."

His father took the skull down from his shoulder. He had never used the word before, or understood its full meaning. But he employed it then: "You're *conservative*," he told his son. To him the word meant those who didn't like to have fun. It also meant—though perhaps no dictionary would back up his definition—people who despised the Raiders. Conservatives, he argued, were those people who wore ties. Raiders fans, he figured, were liberals because they wore T-shirts and jerseys.

"Where do you get these ideas?" his son said before he walked away.

But Adan, the boy who had been born on rowdy Friday, finally agreed to accompany his father, who danced with his son and made his son get in a three-point stance and ram shoulders with him. Ramiro was happy, and he expressed his happiness by ordering a pizza with the works. Instead of eating at the table, he set up his three Raiders TV trays and had his wife and son watch NFL highlights with him.

Game day arrived with the valley layered in fog. Ramiro could hardly sleep the night before, and he woke up early to cook eggs and bacon for his son. They left a little before seven for the four-hour drive to Oakland, *after* they had an argument about how many skulls Ramiro would be allowed to mount on his shoulders. Ramiro decided one skull was too skimpy, but Adan, suddenly furious, said he wouldn't let his father become a spectacle among people they didn't know.

The rest of the drive was uneventful as they traveled through fog that slowly thinned as the sun came out. Near Oakland, however, they became excited as they linked up to a caravan of other cars on the way to the game.

"See how nice people are," Ramiro remarked to his son.

Adan had to agree. "Yeah, they look like crooks, but maybe I'm wrong, Dad."

"Of course you are, Adan." He clenched his fist and yelled out the window, "*¡Vivan Los* Raiders!*"

"*¡Órale! ¡Los* Raiders!" Adan shouted timidly.

Ramiro smiled at his son. He adjusted his eye patch, a habit of his. He glanced in the rearview mirror and admired the skull on the backseat. It was vibrating from the car's motion.

They parked at the Coliseum and walked among fans who were dressed in costumes that made his single skull seem childish. These boisterous fans had skulls that were twice as large, and some of them wore gladiator-like helmets. They had breastplates and shin guards, and faces painted silver and black. Bike chains hung from their thick chests like necklaces.

Ramiro was also amazed by the barbecues. He had expected hamburgers and weenies and bowls of potato chips, but the fans had cooked up feasts. He eyed tri-tip steaks, *carne asada*, and chicken on grills, and pots of soup and soupy beans boiling away. There were lakes of guacamole, colorful salsas, salads, cakes, *pan dulce*, and sodas and beers in chests and plastic tubs like glaciers piled high with ice. Music—rap, soul, and *rancheras*—played from boom boxes.

Ramiro walked among the tailgaters until he heard a voice call, "Hey, come over here with us!" A burly man with a Raiders jersey beckoned him. The man was holding a spatula.

"You mean us?" Ramiro asked.

"Yeah, you two!" the man hollered kindly. "Eat with us."

Ramiro approached the man and they shook hands. The man introduced himself as Chuy. Ramiro then introduced his son, Adan, and Chuy introduced his wife, Gloria.

"Hey, my wife's name is Gloria *también*!" Ramiro said.

Chuy's Gloria was a little heavy, but her heaviness was mostly hidden by her jersey. The jersey nearly reached her knees.

"Where you from?" Chuy asked as he handed Ramiro a soda.

"From Del Rey."

"*¿De veras?*" His eyes got big with exaggerated excitement. "We're from Reedley."

"No way," Ramiro said. He calculated that Reedley was only thirteen miles from Del Rey, and it took an event such as the Raiders versus the Broncos to bring together people who lived within shouting distance. And they would get to know each other over *taquitos* and beans because both parties had seats in the Black Hole.

"This is a trip," Ramiro crowed. He had never used the word *trip* that way before, but, then again, he had never been to a game, either. He brought a chicken *taquito* to his mouth.

"What grade are you in, *mi'jo*?" Gloria asked Adan.

"Seventh," he answered shyly. He was filling a flimsy paper plate with food.

Gloria smiled. "My kids are grown, and so are Chuy's."

Ramiro understood that they had had children with other people, but that was okay by him. *These are modern times*, he thought. *Plus, I don't want to be a conservative*. He took another bite of *taquito*. Lettuce hung from his mouth like hay.

They ate and talked about work, but then blasted themselves.

"*Pues*, what are we doing talkin' about work, *hombre!*" Chuy scolded.

Ramiro agreed. He turned his attention to his son. "My son plays ball."

"Is that right?" Chuy said. He slipped a tortilla chip into his mouth and clamped down on it.

"I play wide receiver," Adan remarked. "I'm not that good."

"Don't say that, *mi'jo*," Gloria corrected sweetly. She was sitting on the tailgate of their Ford Explorer. She was swinging her small, pudgy legs.

"But it's true."

Gloria argued that it wasn't true. She jumped from the tailgate, a motion that rocked their vehicle, and told Adan to go out for a pass.

Adan put down his plate. He took a few slow steps, looking over his shoulder. Gloria, arm cocked awkwardly, threw an orange, which Adan caught neatly. He tossed it underhand back to Gloria.

"See, he's good," Ramiro said with pride.

"Shoot, if the Raiders are down, they might bring you in, son," Chuy said. He chuckled, and his gut wobbled beneath his jersey.

Ramiro smiled. He liked that Chuy referred to his son as *son*. Gloria had called him *mi'jo*. They were good people. They said that they would like to see Adan play, and they exchanged telephone numbers with Ramiro.

While Chuy and Gloria cleaned up, Ramiro hurried back to the car to get his skull. He returned with it mounted on his shoulder.

"I hope it's nothing that you ate, *hombre*," Chuy joked. "But you got a head growing out of your shoulder. Looks like my ex-brother-in-law." Chuy chuckled with one hand on his belly and remarked, "You look real good with that eye patch. Where did you get it?"

Ramiro explained that it was for his injured eye, and a solemn Chuy said, "Me and my big mouth. I thought it was part of your getup." He patted Ramiro's shoulder and cursed the rosebush that had injured him.

They entered the Coliseum and were jostled by fans yelling, "Raiders! Raiders! Raiders!" Ramiro joined the chant and bumped along the tide until they found their seats. He and Adan were in a different row from Chuy and Gloria. But when Ramiro looked up, he could see his new friends.

Chuy waved and asked, "Nice seats, huh?"

"The best, *compa*!" Ramiro marveled at the effort-less use of the word *"compa,"* a word that implied best friend. He realized that he had no best friend and that, if God allowed, he was going to make Chuy his best friend. Ramiro pictured them enjoying a barbecue in his own backyard. Adan would take digital pictures of them arm in arm, and pictures of the two Glorias— his own much taller, much thinner Gloria and Chuy's Gloria in her Raider jersey. If he could get his Gloria to wear even a Raiders cap, then everything would be . . . picture perfect.

The game started with a Raiders fumble, but it was soon three and out for the Broncos. Then it was three and out for the Raiders, and on the next possession, the Broncos scored.

"*Ay*," Ramiro moaned, and looked up at Chuy, who snapped his fingers and yelled, "*¡Qué lástima!*"

"But it's still early!" Ramiro yelled.

The game was a defensive struggle, and by halftime it was 10–3, Broncos. But at the start of the third quarter, the Raiders had tied the game on a kick return. Then the Raiders went up by another touchdown: 17–10. By then the Black Hole had gotten more packed, as fans pushed toward the first three rows of seats. That occurred when the Raiders scored a touchdown and their wide receiver jumped into the crowd in the Black Hole. The crowd pawed him, and the wide receiver pointed a finger skyward.

Ramiro, unable to contain himself, moved to the lower seats, where Chuy was then pressed between two other fans chanting, "Raiders! Raiders! Raiders!" Ramiro didn't care that his skull had been crushed or that someone had splashed soda on him. He didn't care that Adan remained in his seat. He had to be where the bodies were crushing against one another.

"Go, Raiders!" he yelled until his throat was sore. He smiled as he remembered that he had asked his wife to watch the game and to keep her eyes on the television. There was a chance that she might see him. He had also asked that she record the game. *Chihua-*

hua, he thought. *If only I can be on TV . . .* He prayed that his wife had clicked the RECORD button.

Then he got his chance to be on the six o'clock news. It was during the fourth quarter, when the Broncos scored a controversial touchdown. A few rowdy fans from the Black Hole spilled onto the field behind the goalpost. They had begun to throw wadded-up bags of food and cups filled with ice. The security guards yelled and prodded the fans back into the bleachers. But the fans began to push back, and a fan took a security guard to the ground in a headlock. By then the cops had come lumbering toward the commotion and were starting to handcuff the unruly fans.

"Mira, la chota. They're acting all bad!" Chuy yelled.

"¡Estúpidos!" Ramiro found himself shouting. He realized that it was an unfair remark, but he couldn't help himself. "We should help." Ramiro was even further amazed by his bravado.

"You're right." Chuy jumped down onto the field. He walked toward one of the cops. "This is America, man! These dudes are just having fun!"

"No," Ramiro muttered. He wished he hadn't said what he had said, and that his friend hadn't jumped down into the fracas. "¡Chuy! ¡Ven! Get back over here."

A fuming Chuy waved Ramiro off.

Ramiro looked over his shoulder in the direction of his son. But he could see only arms and fists raised, and the Black Hole fans began to jump the rail to help the handcuffed fans bellied out on the ground. The crazed tide suddenly had him falling over the rail and onto the field. He got up unhurt, though dazed. He quickly got into action after a cop began to whack Chuy behind the legs.

"You can't do that to my *compa!*" Ramiro yelled. He then remembered what Chuy had said: "This is America, dude!" Ramiro had never used the word *dude* before. In the melee, he realized that he was nothing like someone born on a quiet Sunday. No, he was like a man born on a boisterous Friday. He looked back into the bleachers. He couldn't locate his son among the fans who were beginning to throw things onto the field.

"*¡Mi'jo!*" he called. "Stay where you are! I'm going to get my *compa!*"

Hundreds of fans from the Black Hole were on the field, and the security guards and the few cops were in retreat. The hundreds, Ramiro among them, were chanting, "Raiders! Raiders! Raiders!"

The football players on the field had stopped to watch the commotion. The Raiders and Broncos were breathing hard, their steamy breaths blowing out of their helmets. They waited with hands propped on their hips.

"Adan!" Ramiro yelled. "Come on down!" Ramiro scanned the bleachers but couldn't find his son. "Adan!"

he yelled again, and would have continued to yell except a cop as big as a defensive back had tackled him in the end zone. He felt like a player with grass in his face and air being pushed from his lungs.

The next morning Ramiro woke up in jail, with his elbows bloody from having fallen during the stampede. Or maybe it was from when the police had marched them roughly to the idling vans outside the Coliseum. They had been driven to the county jail chanting, "Raiders! Raiders! Raiders!"

Raiders Nation. It was its own country inside the United States of America. It had raised a silver and black flag. And if ever there was red on the flag, it was because of blood spilled for a good cause.

Chuy was in the same cell, a hand over his eyes, half asleep. Ramiro lay back on his cot with a sigh. He thought of home and his wife and son—of how, over dinners, he would replay the day for them. Oh, he felt blessed to share a cell with a captured nation of Black Hole fans. He felt the damaged skull on his shoulder and pulled it up to his face. One of the eyes had been poked out.

"Hey, *compa*," Ramiro whispered from the bunk above his new friend.

"What?" a groggy Chuy asked, then smacked his dry lips.

"Do you know if we won?"

Selected Spanish Words and Phrases

ándale: come on

apúrate: hurry up

bigote: mustache

cállate: shut up

casi: almost

¡chihuahua¡: an expression of surprise

chismosa: gossipy girl or woman

chorizo con huevos: pork sausage with eggs

como: as

cómo: how

cómo estás: how are you?

cómo friegan: you are so bothersome

compa: buddy

cuídate: be careful; take care

de veras: really; truly

Dios mío: my God

Doña: madam

dos: two

doscientos: two hundred

el joven es magnífico: the young man is magnificent

ese: that; that one

está: (it, he, she) is

están en la casa: they are in the house

estúpido: stupid

fuego: fire

hace frío: it's cold

hombre: man

huevos con: eggs with

la chota: the police

la mesa: the table

la salsa y pimienta: the sauce and pepper

listo: ready

mami: mommy

me voy: I leave; I go

mi cielo: my dearest

mi'jo/mi'ja: my son/my daughter

mira: look

mis llaves: my keys

mocos: snot

no tengo mis llaves: I don't have my keys

oí nada: I heard nothing

órale: okay; right

pan dulce: sweet bread

papas: potatoes

papi: daddy

pues: then; well then

qué cochino: how filthy

qué lástima, muchacha: what a pity, girl

qué linda chica: what a pretty girl

qué no: isn't that so

qué pasó/pasa: what happened/happens

quién sabe: who knows

rancheras: popular Mexican songs

ruca: girl

también: too

taquito: small taco

tenemos que comer: we have to eat

tía: aunt

vato: guy

ven acá: come over here

ven/véngase: come

vivan: that they live

voy: I go

ya: already

y tus padres: and your parents